BY JOHANNES GÖRANSSON BY SARA TUSS EFRIK BY JOHANNES GÖRANSSON BY SARA TUSS EFRIK BY JOHANNES GÖRANSSON BY SARA TUSS EFRIK BY JOHANNES GÖRANSSON BY SARA TUSS EFRIK BY JOHANNES GÖRANSSON BY SARA TUSS EFRIK BY JOHANNES

THE NEW Q

ISBN: 979-8-9870838-3-3

The New Quarantine is typeset in Freight Display Pro, originally drawn in 2005 by Joshua Darden as a "conscious stylistic device." Titles are set in Karrik, a sans serif created by Jean-Baptiste Morizot for the French open-source type foundry, Velvetyne.

JARANTINE

Sara Tuss Efrik reads Johannes Göransson. She decodes a farce of masculinity, a wounded lover's tragedy, a prison cell of language. Using her knowledge of the occult and pornography, Sara Tuss reads letters that may belong to Shirley Temple and letters that may belong to Louise Bourgeois and letters that may belong to a woman who doesn't belong at all. She finds legs that belong to a spiderlike girl and a confusing sorrow she can't erase. She tries to understand the letters. Is he stuck in the pigsty with all those screaming animals? Can a torso be damaged by loneliness? Is this why he keeps transforming himself into something like an uncle? *You cannot write yourself free; you can only write yourself even more unfree.* That's what she told him, the woman who does not belong at all. She imagines that she's writing violence, a female violence, but she has to take a shortcut, has to use the language of male violence to be able to write the female violence. In that moment when she finally describes her own face, she will bleed. But she's not there yet. She has not yet described her own violence, but she will. She has to reach the end of the quarantine. The word *quarantine* comes via the French *quarantaine* from the Italian expression *quarantena*, which means *a forty-day period*. Sara Tuss has written the definition on a wall in her room. On the same wall she has written: *Come but don't save me*. All these phrases you have gathered: this is a collection of dead lovers or dead children. Your burning horse gallops away from you, the blood dries on the wall. It's a tragic universe of possessions and stalkers. *Welcome home, Johannes*. Bury yourself in your unwritten novels. Everything is set. Now Sara Tuss Efrik will abandon her decoding games and lock herself in Johannes Göransson's quarantine.

THE NEW QUARANTINE WILL DEVOUR YOU

CUCKLING HEN
NARCOTIC UN-MOTHERS
TWINNING FATIGUE
GREEK TEMPERANCE CHOIR
WHAT A BUILDING
INCUBATION TIME VARY DEPENDINGLY
ON THE INFECTIOUS RISK OF THE CURRENT DISEASE
ISOLATION IS A COMPULSION
IN CASE OF SUSPECTED INFECTION
MOIST ANIMALS
DO NOT WIPE OFF
SUCK IN
SORROW ANIMALS
RUINED SEEDS DRIP
THE YELLOW RADIANT INJECTION
BLADERUNNER, VANGELIS
LONGING FOR DEATH
COME AND BRING ME HOME CORPSE
YOU FORCE ME TO LOOK LIKE YOU
COLD SWEET TURKEY
THE LAST COLD DOSE OF TURKEY
PUKE UP A THIGH

THE WORMS ON MY INNER THIGH

FIRST NIGHT

There's no fan in the room. I can't think straight. The heat is sticky, the air is static. The curtains hardly move even though the windows are wide open. Somebody is whistling outside. Somebody else is screaming. A crowd of people are yelling. Their voices grow louder. A piercing siren passes by. I beg Johannes to bring me ear plugs so I can write. He doesn't want to. Our clothes smell bad. I've tried to wash them with hand soap but they're not drying and they smell more and more of mildew. I can't think above the stench.

The gnats are drawn to my wine, they are going to drown in the bottles by morning. I have to follow Johannes's infernal images to get out of here. My ex died two months ago. No one told me what had happened. This is also a farce about the body. His parents and ex-girlfriends will burn in hell. I left lipstick-smeared cigarette butts on his grave. I fantasize about fucking all his friends to be close to him again. It's a wonderful party we have, me and my dead lover, even though I no longer remember what we're celebrating. That we are sober or that we are dead? That there's only one of us left alive? Now how was it done? Take a deep breath. Empty your lungs into the balloon. Leave the balloon at the grave, even though your lover has no need for laughing gas or breathing.

Do you still have air in your dead body? Do you still have a sow left in your dead body? Are you still a sieve? Stuck in your lane? If I bend over your face and at the same time press your chest, can I inhale the air you once breathed? Will you give it back to me? No, you're not the type to give back. That's why I still love you. You hit me and it felt like a kiss. Now I have no more love to give. I have nothing, everything is gone. Or the only thing I have left is the nitrous oxide I inhale when I give birth to all these children. All other breathing seems unnecessary.

One woman has tape over her mouth and she's terrible at dancing. Her name is Shirley. Or that's the name she uses when she writes frightening accounts of history. They are frightening because they claim it's not over, history. Is her other name Elsie? Her sister is frightening because she refuses to tell us what she is doing here. Her name is Louise if I can judge from the writing on the wall. I'm writing this on the wall: *I'm coming for you.* I'm coming for Johannes, but the statement – like all great works of poetry – is open to interpretation. You may think I'm referring to history. Or to the poem. The one about Anti-death. The poem in which I was first dressed in bombazine. From head to toe. Then they shoved it into my mouth. Then I began to see. Not like a sick person, but like a mother. That poem was called New Jerusalem.

Junk Song #2

Rub the skin
from your sternum
polish the bone
use a spoon
to scoop out the monkey
brain the illness teeth
the beak's
intravenous sores

Blessed be the unwashed, the dirt coating the bathtub, the unwashed ones who go to bed with my taste in their mouths, blessed be piss and detergent, boiled needles, piles of ashes, drained cans of cheap beer, tinfoil. Our bathtub must be the ocean of everything. And I live on the butcher's island.

THE NEW QUARANTINE WILL BE LOUDER
THAN ASCETICISM

Then there's silence. Silence has always ruled inside the quarantine. I understand this instinctively. But I also understand instinctively that there are creatures in there that want to destroy the silence. To poison the silence. To name me after its poisons.

Inside the quarantine, all the dialogue is about the body, and what can be done to it. There's a buzz. An environmental disaster. I write *oink oink* on the wall. It's an obscene exit language. I am learning how to translate. All those swarming bodies must belong to the quarantine. The role they are auditioning for must be Anti-death. I'm auditioning for it too.

You don't know that I'm still asleep, and that this sleep is taking place beneath a rusty duvet. That I mumble with flour in my mouth. That I am the bush that burns. I should be the one left at the stake. I can't be burnt. Forests avoid me. Eggs proliferate beneath the rusty duvet. I speak from inside a red flower in an act of baroque self-effacement, the red red glows red. You burned like a flame. The word flame is such a low word. The word glows while you are kneeling bent overturned upside down reversed. You exhale prayers, I hang from a beam. Is this Calypso speaking? Is it Shirley? Is it Elsie? Who? There are those who want to hurt me so I'll give myself a name.

Her.

Let's give the role to her.

Her name is Sara. Her name is video. Her name is Alejandra. Her name is Francesca. Her name starts with A. Her name ends with Z. Her name is Tuss. Her name is Morphine. She plays with spoons. She whistles a tune about spoons – a vein melodye, a tune-tune-tune-out. Her name is Out. His name is In. Drop out. Come in. Knock know who's there? The woman who does not belong.

Come in, whispers Shirley.

You don't have to, whispers Louise

A SHOTGUN WEDDING INSIDE THE RIBCAGE OF THE BOURGEOISIE

Oh mon dieu! Everything washes through me, the smoke from the ashes of the uterus and the stench of vomit. I reshape memories and acts of violence and turn it all into ruins. I hang myself by the noose and watch how flowers grow out of my strangled head, how they multiply and the skulls multiply, all these skulls. History is changed. I don't remember anything – who is the sender and who is the receiver? – except that I would like to rest soon, I have earned my rest, haven't I, a little rest you can still treat me to? I sit under the beams yearning for the ugliness and the man with the belly. I am your hostess. I sit here and send out holograms of Shirley Temple from the exact moment she was exposed to the world. I'm the only one who can see her true age. No one knows that she belongs to me. I'm also the only one who gets to witness her menopause. Together we play with botox and fillers. Do you see how she changes? How she becomes herself? Becomes the world.

I'm exposed by the poem but I was never exposed in real life. I was never murdered in the basement, says Shirley, and I want to believe her but I've read the poems. I know she was exposed like a photograph. I hang beneath the beams, exposed like her, and broadcast the story of her body. My voice – which is the voice of women in Johannes's description of riots and burning meadows – tells me I am filling up the quarantine with bomabazine. Tells me I'm playing a game. *Anti-death*.

Here's what happened to you in the poem about pig slaughter and the unzipped pants: You fell in love with an arms manufacturer's daughter. Before you fled from her, you hid a fist full of Christmas decorations in her dress, maybe as a gift, maybe to get back at her, I don't know for sure. Maybe she was your hiding place. Then you fled straight into the arms of Louise.

You still think of the arms manufacturer's daughter when you feel lonely and want a revolver up your ass. You always return to the uncertainties that have to do with the light, whether it comes from your mouth or ass, whether it's a light at all. I know one thing for sure and that's that Louise's care is not enough for you. When she turns you inside-out, you think about Greek choruses who understand what happens inside the skin. Maybe you just want Louise to accept you for who you are.

Even with her glamorous 50s-style aura, Shirley doesn't know how to dance. It shows. When she does the Twist, it looks like she wants to hurt me. *She wants to hurt you, Sara Tuss.* She wants to hurt every spectator. Every mother. Shirley doesn't want the bomb to go off but Louise tells me it already has. She's making spiders for the aftermath. It's the second night. It's the third night. It's the fourth night. Why all this knocking? It's Shirley, she wants out. *I want her to be me.* The quarantine is where diseases mingle. Hate and love: *You are searching for an entry to the poem, I am searching for an exit wound.*

Repeat: Shirley is a girl. Shirley is a stained pig. Shirley thinks she's a celebrity but she's not. Shirley is a hologram. Shirley gives me his tiara because I meet all her demands of masculinity. The tiara is full of rusty nails. The tiara is my thorn crown. I thank you humbly. She seems to keep track of the story, Shirley, maybe she already knows the end I'm carrying. Shirley applauds my feminine masculinity. She believes in my suffering. How lucky. My suffering is the only thing I believe in. Shirley is not that stupid. Not yet.

I call out to Louise. I ask her to bring me rain water. I know it's toxic, I tell her. I am making Art. Fake art for a fake child's sake. The mother of screams. I'm becoming her in the poem by the American Son. The counterfeit son. I will fuck this poem up but the poem is already inside me. Louise is inside of me. With her spider veil. With her bombazine dress. I can't even see my own face in here. I can see my face in the silver spoon. The quarantine is a kind of factory where I can reshape memories and acts of violence, where Johannes can hang himself in the noose and see how, out of his broken head, flowers grow, proliferate. All these flowers, all these skulls, all this radiation: *Nobody can belong in here.*

EVERYONE BELONGS IN THE NEW QUARANTINE

I hear such strange noises from the Greek chorus. I want to put on that record by Satie that Shirley loves to pass out to. I have passed out to it so often in strange hotel rooms I know every moment with my mouth. Your eros was shaped by fainting in hospital corridors. You have to repeat after me: *Shirley is not a nurse. She is a girl. She is a stained pig.* Shirley thinks she's a celeb but she isn't. Shirley is a hologram that I made for my mother so that she could see that I was safe in Art. Now I'm taking off my mask.

I am Shirley.
I think my sister wants me dead
but she may also want me anti-dead.
The only audition I want to attend anymore
is for the round, powdered girl
who takes every drug. The King and Queen
of Human Suffering. I'm not dumb
I have fucked and been fucked.
I have read the book about tigers
and poisoned trees. The world is
my art. It's only the fourth night
you've been in this factory
and you're already searching
for the exit wound. I'm searching for
the angel with the red wings.
Your zipper is open.

There are enough parasites in this bed to make me royalty. King of milk. Street of thighs. I want to make such a wonderful cake out of your face, Shirley, but I can't bring myself to do it, can't bring myself to live up to your idea of my father. You're a farce too, little thigh cake. Oh Shirley, I could make such a beautiful paradise out of you if you would only let me, I could fill your poem with so many bodies: girls, spotted pigs, runaway children, tortured soldiers. Oh Shirley I could put your silk ribbon in my mouth if it wasn't so damn dirty. Oh Shirley, I'm a pig and you know it and I know you know it. That's why you never leave me. That's why I keep loving you. Because you can't leave me. You are locked in my farce, just as I am locked in yours. I'm only talking about things that make you anxious. I stand in line with the other animals. This is our army. You will not get away.

Shotgun.

[*A shotgun is heard from another room.*]

Shirley isn't safe so she gives me her tiara. I don't want this tiara so I give it to Johannes. Johannes says he wants it. *I want it.* That doesn't sound like him. Is Shirley keeping track of the story? *Yes I am keeping track of the story.* The story of joy. *Anti-death.* Who is the king and queen in this game of hide-and-hide? I am Louise now. I think my sister wants me dead. I know you have tried to make a paradise out of me. An innocence. I play the girl you fucked for drugs. She fucked you in stupid hotel rooms because she wanted to trash your innocence, wanted to expose you to the world. She wasn't a good enough artist to know that it was the other way around. Now the world belongs to you.

Shirley, maybe she already knows the end I'm heading toward.

[*Shirley applauds my suffering.*]

How lucky.

My suffering is the only thing I believe in.

It tells me I belong to the world.

Start over.

Butcher this poem.

For forty nights.

But how can I start over? Take a deep breath. Empty your lungs into the balloon. Leave the balloon for the grave even though your lover doesn't need either nitrous oxide or breathing. Shirley, I'm too tired right now, I can't perform my own farce the way you want me to. You are also a farce, Shirley. You and your sister Louise, who are always fucking up the Christmas ornaments when I try to remember them or when Johannes tries to remember what you did to his riot anatomy with the Christmas ornaments and what you did that made him think about pigs always pigs when he thinks about your violence when he thinks about the violence of capitalism horse-cadaver capitalism and what you did that made him so filthy. It must have been Louise who stuffed that bombazine veil into his mouth.

Oh Shirley, I'm a pig and you know it and I know you know that you will never leave me. That's why I will keep loving you. Because you can't leave me. You're locked up in my ridiculous story and I'm locked up in yours. I only talk about things that make you anxious. I have started numbing my anxiety with alcohol. I stand in line inside Johannes's quarantine. The line is our army. You will not get away.

[Shotgun goes off. This time it sounds closer.]

What was that? What am I going to do with my own wreckage when I'm this lost in the quarantine? What am I going to do with my body when everything seems like carnage and paper roses? Will I ever get out of here? Will I ever want to? You can't leave without me.

I'm eating pork tonight, Shirley. I'll eat your face tonight, Shirley. I'll eat virgin flesh and rotten tissue. I have given you my camera. I asked you to take selfies with it. Raw selfies. Have you taken selfies of your bruises yet, Shirley? Have I kissed your face yet, Shirley? Does your face look worse than my lover's junkie den before he overdosed? Does your face look worse than the time I laughed my own face off? Am I your violator? Am I your ghost? Is this how I'll get close to you? I'm afraid. I'm always afraid. Isn't it written all over my face, Shirley? This place is full of prom queens but the only queen I want is you, Shirley. You are the ghost queen of a porn show that is still taking place. My torso still smells like you.

I bent over your body when I thought you were asleep but you weren't, you were working on a farce about me, I was your moon doll. You were playing the part of the meat, I was playing the part of thieves. Why do you always think that others are doing the stealing? You're through with me but I'm not through with your farce. You touched me and it felt like a kiss. I want to feel that kiss again. I want to butcher this poem.

Louise wants me to cut up the sorrow animal. *Cut it up.* Instead of being a mother, I want you to play the part of the junkie. I don't want to let go of your fingers. My mouth is felled with a silence that obliterates. I hate protest art but I want you to bring my body back from the riots. The crime photos cannot quite ever capture the innocence of my whole body and the fruit smeared on it is too bright. The burnt bombazine looks like spider webs. I'm making protest art. Terrible spring with its terrible seeds. It can't last forever. My silence is a protest against forever. Against death. My silence is an island where we can meet again.

Let me hurt you, whispers Shirley.

But don't let the bomb destroy the garden.

Let the bomb destroy the garden.

I whisper back.

MUMMYLAND

Dear Mum,

Let me make myself perfectly clear: I don't blame you for anything. I've never blamed you for anything. I am in your debt. You gave me life.

You taught me the difference between private and public violence. You taught me about the furious luxury of the quarantine. You gave me a bruise on my thigh that will never go away. Ever since I was born, I've been working on my audition for the quarantine, but I'm still not good enough. I need your help.

The bruise is a riddle of sorts. Beauty is always a riddle. Your toothmarks are the shape of a spider. My thigh doesn't belong to me any longer.

You don't need to ask me any questions. The answer is always the quarantine. The answer is always at war with the question. The question always has to do with inmates and guards. With peepholes.

In my great novel I travel through America. I sleep on a plastic-encased mattresses. I sweat. I wear clothes with obscene phrases written in English. The forests burn as we drive through them – dad and I, Humpty Dumpty and I, Edgar Allan Poe and I – and we drive through them and through them. He fucks whores and I search for another father. I need to buy a new father made of gold. I need to sell him to the highest bidder.

The forests burn, the helicopters burn, the heroes go insane. The footnotes are about victimhood but they sound like love poems to gold. They're a sick excuse. I imagine what it's like to join a mob. To tear down a home for the elderly. I pretend it's war.

It's war. Every morning is the same. I don't show anyone my swollen tits. I might be pregnant. I might give birth to a boy who will have nothing to do with your vagina or your teeth. I wear a funeral gown and look in the mirror. What will war do to me now that it's come at last?

Dear Mum,

I tried calling you but the phone doesn't work inside the quarantine.

I can't take another lie. Once upon a time I looked in the mirror and I saw grimaces so heavenly the mirror cracked. The shards are laughing at me. Laughing at the American boy. They were made for his body. I imagine him with a contorted boy and a broken face. I imagine that the giggling I hear belongs to whores who wear lace and neon thongs.

I've written my name on raw meat. Are you jealous? I'm pregnant with a boy. I wish I had inmates or I wish I was an inmate and the guards were beautiful. I fantasize about teaching them their mother tongue. I would tell them about the difference between public and private violence. I would teach them how to draw copies of my bruise. The spider on my thigh. I would ask them about the master plan.

Why did you bite my thigh? You have questionable taste and all my disguises come from you.

Dad and I drive through the burning forests. We sleep in mansions that are falling apart. The rain leaks in the ceiling and drips on my face and on my swollen tits.

When I sleep it's like parrots are singing inside me. It doesn't end. Are you jealous? It's like I'm praying. The butterflies and night-flies and dragon-flies get in my hair. It's like I haven't been born at all yet. But I'm happy. I call myself hyacinth girl, tulip girl, stalking horse, heaven's whore. I dream about raw meat. I picture you sleeping on raw meat. I want every charge against me to be true.

I have two sisters: Louise and Shirley. Louise has drawn spiders on Shirley's body, which is the most beautiful body I've seen because she is always clean. She will give me a new name.

Dear Mum,

My purse is full of blood. The sisters are sitting at my feet. Death has a certain fashion status. Especially in the afternoon when the sisters move around. They've hid the cat gold in one of the pillows. In another they have puked. You will rest your head on one of those soft soft pillows and I will rest my head on America.

The distant giggling doesn't seem to come from a person. A little further in, there's an open gate, but it doesn't seem to belong to any building. Johannes is a lie. He doesn't belong in this language. He belongs to a girlish heaven.

Dear Mum,

The American Boy doesn't know my name. Sometimes in his diatribes, I play the part of Death. It's my most beautiful role. I wear a harness. I dictate the terms of surrender. I have many children. They provide me with absolution. I provide them with poisoned milk. I give them to the world.

Shirley and Louise: Those are the two sister but the American Impostor gets them confused and calls me by their names because that's who he's thinking about when he speaks. But most of all he knows me as the Spoon Woman. I belong to the world.

Tomorrow I'll give myself a new face. Even Pa won't recognize me as we drive through America, through the burning forests, a heap of Amaryllis Belladonna in my lap, the red flowers scattering all around the car. *There was glory, we were stars.* Pa is played by the American boy. He's not American. He's wounded, almost flower-like. He is bleeding from the side of his torso. He doesn't know how to use a shovel properly. He thinks he's digging for the truth. But most of all he wants the Spoon Woman to tell him what the car radio tells her about his weak, weak body. It tells me how to put out my cigarette.

Dear Mum,

Tomorrow I'll give myself a new name. Even Pa won't recognize my name as he drives me through America, through the burning forests, a heap of Amaryllis Belladonna in my lap, the red flowers scattering all around the car. There was glory, we were stars. Pa is played by the American boy. He's not American. He's wounded by flowers. He is bleeding from the side of his torso. He doesn't know how to use a shovel properly. He thinks he's digging for the truth. Most of all he calls me Spoon Woman.

Dear Mom,

The name Spoon Woman comes from a postcard I bought at the Kiasm Museum in Helsinki in 2004. The ice cream dripped and I wanted to fuck my teacher because of the way she handled the silverware in the cafeteria. The next time I'll have the chance to fuck her I'll probably be too old. The next time I will be someone else. The color scale of my postcard is much lighter than the version I find online. The internet reproduction looks colder, overexposed. The woman on the postcard is nailed to the wall with a spoon. I belong only in an overexposed world. The title of the artwork is *Brand (Fire)*. One day I will send a copy to my teacher. I will send one to you too, dear mom, and I will draw in my genitals.

Dear Johannes,

Classic Literature is about the lonely island, the red flower and the synthetic woman. The Spoon Woman is a woman who cannot articulate her own insights. All phrases are lies but on the lonely island the shame runs out of her as through holes in a sow. She speaks through the sow. Ie she doesn't speak at all. The blood makes a red flower on the ground. This is her silence.

The quarantine is one such island. She lives here. The Spoon Woman. What does she want? The spoon is how I shut her up. I cover her face with the spoon. For now. Can you see the distorted view of yourself, Johannes? It's reflected in her spoon. Which version of your face will you choose, Johannes? The concave one or the convex one? Bring both faces to the audition for the quarantine.

The Spoon Woman will speak again and again. In the quarantine her shame is powerful. It's not classic literature, it is pig literature. It is a cut-like-a-pig literature. The-pig-screams-like-a-stung-pig literature.

Shame is powerful and it has already destroyed the quarantine. Why would anybody enter this quarantine of pig-screams and shame and dead daughters? To find the silver spoon of course. Why would anybody want to attack this quarantine? To find the woman of course. Why would anybody read a poem about this butchery? As an instruction manual of course. How to never fully survive.

Calypso is our goddess, the one who rules the island. But is it time for Calypso to go to bed now? Calypso shy girl the protozoa's Ulysseus the female beast's Odysseus, I bow before her and her secret island which is Ulysseus's quarantine. The Calypso girl will be played by Shirley Temple with her mouth taped shut. I will be played by Louise Bourgeois fucked up on drugs. The quarantine will be razed and rebuilt for 40 days. This is the tenth night. I have already rebuilt it twice. Your turn.

NEW JERUSALEM

The Ballad of a Mother

Her purse is full of blood.

She stutters into the phone.

She says: That's not my army.

But it is. It is.

We are.

The witch hunt does not work as a metaphor if the reader's own position has not been transgressed. The fish bait rots in the pool. My starvation exercises don't work without whiskey either. I know so many arts! Come look at my art! The quack and his books cannot be burned at the stake unless his apathetic mythology is also burned with him. I am the quack who juggles flesh and words. Still, I need to fix the lock. Still not done with the pork. You have a porky face when you put that makeup on, Shirley, and I'm your counterfeit lover. *Quack quack.* We blame it all on Louise, we do. She is our calculating machine, our crystalline material. She rules us with an iron fist. She is our order, we circle around her as if she were our black sun. So what do we do with the last balloon? It's from a black and white movie about Elsie. I need to watch that movie again before I write the autobiography of the 20th century. All that sleepwalking. I need to make up my torso so it looks more like a torso and less like a prison break. I contain so many accidents in a row, butchered pearls on a thread, it never ends. Apply my mascara with a swan feather. Push Louise back in a wheelbarrow. Cut me up. BANG. Bury me in your bed and I'll find the holes in your body even if I'm blindfolded. I slaughter the parasites because they are allowed to be closer to your body than I ever was. This is my ongoing act of revenge. I use the animals as props because they are made of meat and therefore potential germ hotbeds. I dress in the American flag when I walk through the desert. It's my prom dress. Don't laugh at me, don't cry for me, save your tears. I'm the son of a liar.

Fortune says: return home, burning child, return home.

That's what it says because I was born on the border. On the other side of the border: toxic fumes, cold developer fluids, tundra frost, lunar cold, frozen life, the Scandinavian shadow side.

It's from the shadow side the angel appeared. The angel with the shotgun. The overdosed lover is a hieroglyph. The junkie mother is a secret. The parrot goes *die die*. The Fentanyl goes *live*. Calypso screams *live*. Everything I say means *hate*.

I'm afraid.

I'm always afraid.

Isn't it written in my face, Shirley?

It's written in milk on the butcher's paper: You're afraid. The strippers told me. The shot-gun gave it away. Because I'm so cadaverous with my insect sounds and shot horses, I have to talk to Louise in code. In this corrupted immigrant code, I have to bleed from my hands. I have to act like I'm attacking my own face with peonies. That's where the insect sounds originate. There and in my pale pale skin. There and in my Calypso song about women's bodies. There on *Death's Island*.

I ask her who got here first, her or Shirley.

It was me she tells me.

I could bring you into screens, says Louise. I could cover your virgin skin with rotting peonies. I would not glorify you, not even if you were an angel, she explains. I would never find value in glorifying or even transforming the tools you use. I'm a virgin and I take selfies when I'm high. I love cake too. I tell her that I am a kind of virgin and I am eating a kind of cake and I have bruises kind of tonight. I take selfies of my bruises. Especially the ones on my inner thighs.

Sara Tuss tells me to take otheries. Don't take selfies all the time of the bruises on your thighs, she says. Please just give me one more fake news about yourself instead. That's what she says. It's a beautiful afternoon to hang yourself from a beam, says Louise. I tell her I'm a virgin and I hate the taste of cake. It's a beautiful day to violate the rules of the quarantine, says Louise and Shirley tells me I am full of class hatred. I tell her that I hate her. She tells me about the angel and Elsie's balloon but it's all lies. I want to know about the shotgun, about her motives. All Shirley tells me is about junk.

Even Louise doesn't know how old Shirley is. Age functions differently in the quarantine. Some figures are never even born in the quarantine or only live for thirteen days. They almost belong to me. To my party. I'm the only one who will witness her menopause. She doesn't know how much she will change. How she will become herself? Overall, I think her most elaborately bodily feature is her drowned violets. I acknowledge everything as the raw material for my self-portrait as a mother.

I hate you right back

I want you to pose like an angel by the window, Elsie.

I doubt the dramaturgy of all other porn shows except my own. Unlike your translations, my show takes place in the sun sun sun.

I am committing my body to the buzzing of the quarantine, not because
I hate my body but because I want things to end. To burn like sugar. I'm
hungry in this poem.

You are always giggling like girls in your poems because you have sold out.

THE NEW QUARANTINE HAS BEEN SOLD

THE NEW QUARANTINE OPERATES ON THE
PRINCIPLES OF SACRIFICE

Shirley speaks to me from a place that sounds like riots. Sara Tuss writes on the walls of the factory: The pools are too empty. Louise: There are so many tricks in the body! In this ground zero for figurative language, I will look like there is snow on my eyelids. Shirley will look spasmatic in the snow. I will show Sara Tuss how to become a new human. Sara Tuss, in this terrible spring, will become a new human, a kind of duchess next to the counterfeit staging of Shirley's body. I will become a new human. A prop human.

You're already a prop.

You think the gun is the prop but it's you.

I DON'T HAVE A GUN

Shirley chases me through the quarantine because I have a foreign body and it must be neutralized. Shirley: I am always asking you to end these poems. I hate my body and I want it to be quiet when I work. It doesn't work. Sara Tuss has come to watch me perform arson. Louise: Sara Tuss has written too much on the wall. She has to eliminate some of the old dream if she wants to survive her own graphomania. Survive Art: I can't do it. The sweet daughter that was killed: she has cured my modernity.

MODERNITY IS INCURABLE
BUT THE DISEASE IS CLEAN

Louise is everywhere this terrible spring with her death musicals. I wanted to clean myself, get rid of myself, but instead I've made her the star of this quarantine.

I've read the writing painted on the wall of the emptied swimming pool: *Return home, burning children, return home.* Lies written in my mother tongue. The subtext is that I was born on a border. On the other side of the border: poisonous vapors, chilly photographic fluids, tundra frost, moon cold, petrified life. That's the shadow side. The mother side. I don't believe it. I'm the author of the lie. Cut my tongue off. Let them eat it, the rabble. It's the truth. Shirley can tell you I'm right. You are catching me red-handed. Paint all over my skin. Paint all over Sara Tuss's skin. Right after I puked last night, I wrote: Why won't they throw away the key? I only have 34 more nights in this spring palace of tainted boundaries.

Your porno metaphors don't work unless you actually touch my locket. Within it I carry my dead lover's incinerated ashes. Pornography has to hide something or it reveals that all pornography is a fraud. Pornography is based on the promise of a reveal. When I'm Shirley with the incinerated letters or when I'm Shirley of the starvation exercises I'm revealing ashes. I'm baiting you in the drained swimming pool. My starvation exercises don't work without the right flesh and the wrong words. Pornography doesn't work without metaphors. I can hear you crying. I have to improve the lock but I'm not through with your pork yet. I have to see Louise. I have to see what she can do to your body.

Come and watch me do the Louise. Come and watch me write a novel about narratives that end in death. Come and dry my tears with a thin scarlet handkerchief. Come and watch me act like a charlatan when you're pigging out, Shirley. But I'm not your charlatan. I'm Louise's charlatan. I'm devastated and she's pretending I'm at war with my masculinity. Let's blame everything on Louise. Yeah, that's what we'll do. She understands why we're so full of self-hatred. Why I want to incinerate the parts of me that both makes me the most human and most monstrous. She's painted a black sun on the last balloon, the one stuck in the telephones wires in the black-and-white movie from the Weimar Republic. So what should we do with the balloon now that the 20th century has already taken place? Let's take that money shot again. Louise has cast me as the lost girl. The absent girl. She whistles me out. It's a movie about the 20th century. About pigs. Hygiene. We can't talk, there's no sound in this movie. Either because she's dead or because her dead lover's back.

Nature boy, my lover is never coming back. This poem is about the fact that he cannot come back even if I fill his orifices with pomegranate seeds. Even if he sings the most beautiful song Shirley has ever sung for money. Louise doesn't strike deals. Not even with you. Even if I paint your torso to make it look more believable when the music starts to drag. I need to figure out why your poetry is dismissed as pornography and why your body has been portrayed as a site of violence when all you ever do you do softly. I'll use the finest, most beautiful strokes. I'll describe you as something that breathes at night. I'll wear the ballgown. The mother of all ballgowns. I'm the mother of all liars. They all tell me you're laughing at me. Me and my pigged-out body. In this movie I'm Louise with the spider veil over my face. Do the Louise for me.

[*He does the Louise with the veil over his face. His body is highly penetrable. His voice is beginning to tear. Give him your rifle. Give him your handjob. Pig him out in front of the smashed camera. Take a crack at him.*]

[*She does the Louise for him. She looks more deadly in the blue light from the broken window. Her movements are more spastic than expected. She evokes somehow the beauty of flawed tailoring. The stitches.*]

BANG

I'll find the secret about the angel. I'll find it in the locket. I'll let the parasites out. A swarm pornography. Swarm meaning. Permit me to be closer to your body than I have ever been. Permit me to start a revenge campaign against the body: slogans against sex. I want to be against sex with you. Our eyes will be austere. I'll go there with the soiled dress. I'll wear an American flag with bacteria on it. You can cut me in your prom dress. I can photograph you in the slaughterhouse. I'll do the Shirley if you promise not to laugh. Not to cry. I'm such a liar. You're such a mother. Way down in the roots lies my daughter. She belongs to Louise now.

You: I have eradicated the woman with the spoon.

Me: Bring her back.

You: I can't –

RETINA, IGNITE

The boy never turns off the storm inside, never comes down from his communion with insoluble inner deities. Is he hysterically screwed-up now? Is he high? Is there something wrong with him? The girl laps it all up, licks his arms like a thirsty kitten. Hepatitis is cured with Pegasus, a new cure named after a horse. The flying horse cleans the girl's blood.

Hepatica Nobilis. Liverwort. *Blåsippa*. It's Sweden's' national day today. Subcutaneous injections for nine months will clean the girl. Nutritional drinks. Withered muscles. The lovely kingdom of sickness. The girl doesn't even weigh 40 kilos. She wasn't even invited to her boyfriend's funeral. The girl wants to blow his parents' heads off.

A new life, new times, new blood, new books, new seeds, new children, new islands, new auditions, new sisters, new deaths. The new quarantine. What is Anti-death? It sounds promising, tempting. Who can invent their own death? Not even God can invent his own death. The girl plays a game with the poem: Anti-death. That's what she said, the girl who doesn't belong. All these phrases written for dead lovers and imaginary fetuses. You call your thigh Anti-death.

Write your brittle soul under the influence. The chemicals in your body are always better than the drugs you buy, that is if you have enough courage to extract drugs from your own cocktail. You are not a human being, you are a condition. You are being poisoned by your own perceptions. Don't spoil the cocktail mix. Sometimes you have a greater need for self-medication. Don't disappoint me. Move through your own words, see yourself in all the rooms, get stuck in your own sty, captured for forty nights. Then move through someone else's words, get slaughtered in all the rooms. You cry in the shower. You're scared. We don't need any bars on the windows. What we need is a greater space for internal bleeding. There is a lot of giggle-giggle inside God. Many feet kick beneath the taut skin.

Listen to how they dig: sand, worms, underground labyrinths, cadaver perfume. Listen to the ornate torso. Listen to my lethargic voice. Listen to the parodic hymns: insects beneath the skin, waxy body, the amorphous structure of translation, we do not belong here, we make the nature of the translation unnatural. Inside a quarantine, every sickness becomes a revelation. Outside the quarantine you can hear the swarm taking place inside my beautiful bag. Don't open the door to the allegory. The funeral has begun.

Stop pathologizing everything, says my husband in all seriousness. It's Sweden's national day and I'm finally going to give him a daughter.

But my picked-apart anatomy does not really look like it did yester-day. Feathers brushed my sucked nipples. It's a repetitive joke I tell to my husband, but also to confuse diligent readers who may have ugly fantasies about stabbing my landscape open because they can hear my swarm heart inside. Listen! My chest makes that sound, it's a fleeting pleasure because it's squandered. Most people like to masturbate to visuals, but I like to say that my arms are flocked. Lambs devour the tigers and I learn to speak English like an architect who builds burning barns. The glass is almost unbreakable, the pearls almost inedible. *My face is almost innocent in October.* Violent gods almost take place at the same time as naked bodies are hosed off for the party. My face is the face of rage for the party. My revulsion is the antidote.

Your husband is played by Louise. She fools him into trying to put on a shirt without an opening for his head. She wants him to re-enact another Greek play but he's too busy fucking you in the filthy bathtub. You're giving birth to his daughter. The Greek classics depend on incest. Just like the small chamber plays that take place on street corners, in basements, in shitty hotel beds. Your husband is being played by Louise in selfies. She selfies herself in vulnerable positions. She pretends to play with rabbits. She speaks the mother tongue. She lies to you about spoons. She's going to nail you with the spoon. She's going to spoon you out, Spoon Woman.

My husband knows everything, but he always blinds himself, even when I dampen his anxiety with alcohol. But one has to be careful when one has become a mommy. Since my husband can't do it, it's up to me to teach the kids how to find the tunnels and how to do the best to extinguish the fires in them. Maybe it's also my task to finally bury them. It's tricky to teach them about darkness. I was hoping they would take care of it themselves.

We always get stuck on the wrong side of the tunnel.

My husband refuses to listen to my prophesy.

The walls are usually not this thick when the rooms are used for interrogation.

How do we log out?

Thirty-two more nights to go.

I want all this messianic torso-and-pony show to take place in the eye of a needle, that's the problem with me. Everything fits in that eye. I want to tear up the quarantine with a needle. The 9th night has bedded us down. The 10th night's nightly purpose is to let us out in the world, despite the fact that the infection will never be healed. I want to drive those innocent counterfeits down the well and further down to the city's tunnel system. My heart is burning. Yes, a child is dead. Two children are dead. Does that mean we have to be spoonfed by a virgin army? Does it mean that my iconophilia will be cured? That we will be virgins again? I have to start cleaning, I think to myself as if I were covered with sloppy pearls and insect husks. I have to get rid of all these gaudy masks. For the sake of my reputation, I have to eliminate all these little skeletons. The problem right now is all these beautifully distorted birds. Come in my chosen birds! I'm playing mob with my girlfriend. With poetry. The girls are playing a game with the poem. They call the game Anti-death. It never ends. Let's set fire to the dolls that are stuffed with rice and white feathers. We're self-incinerating the 21st century in order to never make it out of this terrible hour. We're incinerating the 21st century in order to become human again. What a disappointment. I see the writing on the wall. It's written by refugees. They're not human, it's written on the wall. The cursive looks immaculate.

When I say that I try to reconstruct nights I've spent inside this quarantine, I mean I try to drown my horse and when I say that God is violent, I mean: there is no room. I mean: it's an allegory about the state. In the state of emergency, we become both human and not human at all. We become poets. We are locked in the factory with all these words. Human, not human. Human, not human.

Not human, not human, not human, not human

This quarantine is the kind of salacious place that is meant for the shooting of horses. For rubbing one's torso with gasoline. The intravenous trafficking of fluids makes a nauseating sound. Even I will be cleaned off in this poem. If the bluebells don't work, I'll try the casino. I'll try the one true substance in the most beautiful bullet paradise of the 21st century: Hate. I love this room. Everyone else is dead. Radiant. I wear my hate on my sleeve. Cut it up, cut it up. Shove it in my mouth. Call it Anti-death but we both know how this quarantine works. The body has us in a bind, it's such a terrible place for inventing futures. It's such a beautiful place for endings, but the narratives all collapse.

I don't remember anything about myself. Just the grace of being able to cling to my own poison. To make a hiding place in my own wordless essence. The sky smells like blood, looks like it is being torn up. You're walking around, dripping blood and cum. Stinking of sweat. The trauer-spiel has begun. It's about Anti-death. It has to be because otherwise we will never clean up this mess. The mess is the Anti-death. The hygiene is violence. We use the mess. To write the text. It starts, *It was the best of times to be sad and the worst time to be naked.* In the quarantine, we undress thousands of bodies every minute. It's a kind of pornographic sublime. It's all about the numbers. This place was built in the twentieth century but will be torn to shreds in the 21st.

I want to marry my mouth to nonsense.

I've heard it's dangerous to translate words that don't mean.

I think there's an ecological dimension to it.

THE LANDSCAPE IS INFECTED,
THE FLOWERS ARE TOO RED

I sort legs in the abandoned factory. I keep the pearls soft inside my mouth. I keep the hares hidden. I clean a woman with gasoline. She's played by Shirley and her mouth is covered up and her hands have been smudged out. It's hard to tell what she wants to do with the hares. The hares are kept protected but they will also choke in the end, like all things hidden. I thought they had sharp teeth but they have no teeth at all. They do not even have mouths, says Shirley, but I don't know if she means the hares or the flowers (blazing stars, torn wings, culver's root) she hands me as a bribe. No I won't give you the hares. I won't give you the hare bells or the blood bells. You want me to bleed, Shirley, for these flowers. I want you to tell me a fairy tale about starving children. You need to get out of here, not because I'm guilty or innocent, but because the show must go on. The flowers must burn in my hands. Louise must run the show with a silver hammer. Louise must use the shards to write on my arms. Louise must write the name of my daughter with her favorite shard. Shirley must have a mouth in which to put Sara Tuss's silver spoon. She must become the Spoon Woman if we are ever to figure out what is taking place in this quarantine. She must show us the dangers of getting out.

Louise: Sorrow is what draws you into a place like this

Louise: Force me to look like you.

Louise: Ask me for your language back

Louise: Tell the Fortunate Son I live in his room now.

Louise: I have written him letters about nature

Louise: Nature is a house haunted by toxins

Louise: Translation is a house haunted by nature

Shirley: No translation is what haunts nature

Louise: What haunts poetry?

Sara Tuss: Morpheus

Johannes: Anti-death

Louise: The Mother Tongue

Shirley: Elsie

You have to go into debt in order to speak to the dead.

THE SECRET DIARY
OF A PIG CIRCUS

There are no stairs in the factory but there's a girl in here and her name is Elsie. Elsie, Elsie why do you paint pictures of balloons on the wall? Are you an angel or a shotgun? I don't know what she looks like but I paint her portrait of on the wall. I paint her green because I want her to be alive. The picture shows children stepping out of boxes, worms curling beneath their pajamas. Green. Green is lovely. I painted her green because it's a lovely color. I wrote this poem in green on a floor in a slaughterhouse while you were editing your documentary about emigration. About our deadly relationship, what Louise will eventually turn into her own art (since she is the kind of woman who makes art out of bombazine). Before I came here, someone edited a movie about distances. Perhaps it was Louise's own film. Perhaps it was about Elsie, perhaps it starred Shirley. Perhaps it was a film about Europe sleepwalking into war or about the great American beauty pageant. The film's work title: *Estrangement*. The film's methods: Disautomatization. The object should be to perceive as ignition, not recognition. I piece it together from the leftovers on the floor. The pig blood is on the close-ups, my fingers smearing the image of the man who is trying to spit out everything. He looks so familiar I want to cut him out. Oh, our exhausted eyes! I'm that man. I want to spit you out of me.

Green. I spit out green. Green was still the color of my eyes when I wrote *The Diary of a Pig Circus*. Green. The color has not yet spread on my mother's retina. Green. Green fields. Open thighs. Charley horse. *Crash boom*. And it felt like a kiss. Green is lovely. Green is a poem about murder. Green is the devil's invention. I use a guitar string to paint a naked body green because I want the melody to stay clean and the woman to stay alive. I use chalk to write the word on the wall of the factory: Green.

She is alive.

There are no stairs in the factory but a woman is in here and her name is Elsie. She looks green in the light from the black sun. I painted her green. I painted my torso to look more expensive, and I painted the bullets green because metal cannot hurt me. You cannot hurt the sleep-walker. I cannot hurt Shirley any longer. She's too modern now. Too beautiful, too violent. It feels like a kiss. A green kiss.

Play with the riddle. Play with an archaic though popular diction. Oh! How will we wash our eyes clean? Do you really need the retina to be sterilized? So many demands, Louise sighs and washes the liver-stains from her hands in an attempt to make herself a master of this artwork. Then she pulls down her unwashed panties and sits down and pisses her latest sculpture while listening to Shklovsky reading *The Diary of a Pig Circus* or *Zoo, letters not about love*. Her piss turns the metal green. Her kisses make my arms more modern than the prom dress we are tearing into pieces for the final showdown with the twentieth century.

The letters are never about mom. They are about green.

Every answer is so baroque when you're far from home.

Every question is about cruelty and the human body.

Something tells me I am looking for a bomb.

Something else tells me I've been invited to kiss you.

Oh, how laughable the world looks with all these mothers in furs! Oh, how ridiculous the world looks with all those spider legs. Oh, how ridiculous the world looks with all those stuffed nylon stockings. When I read your poem, it's like my uncle shakes me. Uncle! Here! Touch me. Here. Here. Here. Huh? Am I really that disgusting? No, it's because I'm so cold, I yell back as I look at my own scarred stomach.

Then I look at my arms which are scarred and skinny and shivering. Everything will be settled out on the sidewalk where the world is even colder than in here. The scars will be erased. Do you want my broken fist? It's actually my brother's broken fist, but he's no longer in need of a broken fist. I hope the emptiness eventually turns into an animal, but a different kind of animal, perhaps even a human being. The final figure in my landscape painting is a woman leaning back, balancing a cool spoon on her face. It seems like she could have calmed your nerves if not for the pervasive stench of oven gas and the sensation of sharp metal needles that have not yet been swallowed. Had it not been for the holes. They leak. It's full of strange matter, this quarantine. A strange matter enters the quarantine through the woman's body. She's so beautiful I have to wear rubber gloves to enter her mirror. I have to wear a green face.

It ends with a shuddering animal. The perfect human inside me is shaking. The hare shakes. The uncle shakes. Uncle! How are you? Has nothing ended yet? Distance is the only image of salvation I can cling to. I'm talking about recreation again. Yes what? Relaxing activity? The scar on the stripper's belly is actually quite appealing. A kind of recovery. Mothers in fur. The new animal. This scene will be another failure of the nerves. I am not capable of transforming myself. Not even by your hands, Louise, no matter how much you knead me. No matter how much it feels like a kiss. Shirley won't change no matter how much I kiss her. No, my pyre is not made for birds or hares, it was made for herds and Rome and nursing wolf mothers and forgotten human children and a civilization in a state of crisis, so I am forced to erase my own language. If I had my choice, I wouldn't even be here. I would be far from both Shirley and Louise. Why did you bring me here? If I wasn't here, I would paint a woman with a leash around her neck. *Woof woof.* There she is, *Mother Bitch*.

Listen. No, listen! Shut up sir, shut up! She – a nineteenth-century ghost in a high-necked blouse and tight skirt listening to jubilant witches – is already on a trip. She has brought her dog that back to life. With a poem. Written in green with a spoon. Written in green on her arms. I give her what she wants and then some. I give her even more. I kiss her and it feels like an invitation: to be perfectly silent.

Louise: I have seen pictures of little birds that drink the blood of swans by burrowing their beaks through the swan's white plumage.

Shirley: I have seen images that looked like corpses, and corpses that looked like swans.

Louise: You are making translation mistakes again, sis.

Shirley: It's what I do, sis

Louise: My emblem is the spider.

Shirley: My emblem is Sara Tuss.The video.

Louise: My sister Shirley.

Johannes: My sister Video.

Sara Tuss: My sister Elsie.

You have to speak to the living in order to remain silent when the cops
ask you about your hands.

Death melts on my tongue and now we are out in the open.

Do you also rage against the gods?

Is your hair as tangled as Medusa's?

Were you born on the bottom of a lake?

Is there no end to your tunnel?

Did you crash here from outer space?

What did you say?

I have snake spit.

NEW JERUSALEM

A LITTLE PROM NIGHT INTERLUDE

Louise is jealous of our night, she always has been. She is the kind who wants to own the night but no one has taught her that you do not own the night, the night owns you. That is what the Spoon Woman sings to us. Shy Girl. Her song is a spell for us, and spells always spread out like skirts on the floors of maternity wards. The mother has been poisoned by fertilizers or fertilized by poison. She has never understood that our Louise, who wants to own everything, wants to own the mother's poisonous story. Louise also wants to own her own father, her father's stories, her grandfather's novels, her great grandfather's confessions. She even wants to own her father's betrayals. She wants to make sculptures of his body, sculptures in which he looks pregnant and his gun looks loaded. He could give birth to a child, a child like you.

Maybe Louise owns the factory and wants pictures of us fucking like we were in a black garbage bag. Are there spider-legs in the bag? Return to her what she refers to as her stolen belongings. She's our landlady, isn't she?

Did you inherit those blood stains, Shirley? Are you hysterical now? Your extreme hyperactivity amazes me. The aimless, repetitive, stereotypical way you move deserves an audience. We will exhibit you at Royal Albert Hall, Shirley. This garbage bin is a bargain. It is, right? The winter is sparkling white and it makes the blood spots buzz. Are you really scared of doves, Shirley? I own a terrible collection of dove-like objects. I never thought so many different parts could fit into my mouth. I've grown bitter. I am leaving to find the lost parts again. Are you full now? Yes, pretty full. Shirley? Why are you gasping for air? Your muscles are tense. Is that because of the hares inside? Are you trying to perform nothingness by lying there in your bed all catatonic? Are you a stupor, little Shirley? I already know one person in such a stupor and you're not him.

[Shirley goes all like catatonic in the bed.]

YOU HAVE TO USE YOUR HANDS TO SPEAK TO MONEY,
IT CANNOT HEAR YOUR VOICE.

(When they come here to stuff their fingers in my engine, I'll be far gone. I'll drag my mechanical masterpiece through the woods as if I were the only one who could save the dead children from the fire. I break their legs. They look like doves without wings. Nobody looks at me anymore. The End.)

THE AUDITION

If I agree to do their audition it will pay off in the end, that's what they say, whether I get the part or not it will pay off. Regardless, it will be good for my career. That's what they say. The role? No clue. I don't know. I'm just going to sit there, in a bare room, on a simple chair, with no clothes on. I'll hide my face. And I will whisper. I do not remember. Something about death. I don't remember. Huh? I don't know. They disappeared from the room. I was left alone in the room. The quarantine. They call the room the quarantine. It was freezing cold. Really crazy. I shook, like a naked animal. What kind of naked animal? I don't know. How many naked animals are there? I didn't know what they wanted from me. So I sat there. I just sat there. And shook. Teeth rattled. Like this. Judgment? I do not know. Were they in another room? They filmed everything with the surveillance camera, right? You've probably watched the film? You should watch it. It should count as evidence. I'm a famous movie star after all. What the hell am I doing in this rat hole? What movie was I auditioning for? I never received any information about it. I didn't think about it then, I was so strangely forgetful back then, but afterwards, well now I can see it all clearly.

She said she would be alone. The one who calls herself Louise. Haven't you caught her yet? Then the second appeared, then the third. Their names? Shirley and Elsie. Three very evil women who really did everything to ruin my life since I met them. They have done everything to ruin my career and wipe out my hard-earned fortune. The first certainly called herself an artist. She looked more dead than alive. Dressed in mink from head to toe. The other movie star. Since childhood, she claimed. Her face was bombed. The third claimed to be a poet. I don't remember anything about her. She appeared so unclear. By force they brought me to an island. What sneaky women. From the quarantine a door led to another room. They asked me to get in. Everything glowed ultraviolet. It was a strangely decorated room. It was more like one big solarium. The three evil women had placed palm trees in the corner and a pile of sand in the middle. There was also a children's pool, it was full of clear blue water. In some pots they had planted red poppies. A hammock floated in the air. They called me spoon woman. I haven't taken heroin in thirteen years! They said I would give birth to stillborn fetuses as punishment for once wishing I was unborn. Honestly, they are obsessed with me! They're stalking me! And me who is so naive and forgiving. Well, I always have been. I would have fled while I could. I would have run away to another city, started working as a waitress. I look good in short skirts. And a neat badge with a name across my chest, that would look nice. What's my name? No, I can't say that. I live under a secret identity. The three evil women are still looking for me since I escaped from their artificial island. I'm writing the book of my life. I'll hang them out, expose them. The whole world will see this sattyg. That is my mission. To warn the world about the three evil women. They don't deserve me.

THE KISS

Calypso says I have come home. That I am finally back where I belong. She says, *Belong here*. The apartment is located opposite an educational institution. This is Calypso's backdrop. Flies float lazily over the cutting board. In the nothingness of our farce, I am a Spoon Woman because my skull is a spoon. Please mirror yourself in the convex part. Finally, you become a millimeter bigger than you really are. If you turn the tables, you shrink beyond recognition. Never forget that Calypso is your stage master.

Build a cage. If you're a cheerleader, hide the vermin in your outfit. If there's no end in sight, wipe the blood from the nozzle. Just give thanks and receive the gift. The woman who can no longer spell her own name – the end has always been close to people like her – is a she-animal, but you remain inarticulate and weightless. I'm a touch animal. I don't like to be touched because I'm an animal and I have a body. It embarrasses me. I belong in a museum. Or a protest. Against touching. I've built this museum from scratch. I've been more productive in here than any-where else. Terrible. The new quarantine that has taken the place of the old quarantine. Its nightmare seeds are in my mouth. I'll spit them out.

I have tricked everyone, including myself, and I have tortured Shirley. But I underestimated Louise. They were both obviously being burned at the stake while I was articulating my final thoughts about the relationship of sound and image, gender and violence. I took a shortcut and gave them each a new name. But Louise's name was already counterfeit. I wanted to spit it out, but she spit me out instead. Like a mistake. Elsie? I don't know any Elsie.

I have to be carefully wrapped in plastic in order to speak. Shirley Temple and Louise Bourgeoisie: I can't remember why they are here. What happens when it's a woman who enacts verbal violence? When it's the violence that enacts the woman? When her language becomes a disease. The violence can never be a symptom of that disease. The violence is an expression of her humanity. Where did the red flower go? Into an insectoid dream about the body. Oh Mother.

I dream that I'm crawling around with a bag full of spoons. I'm the cheerleader with vermin in her armpits. The innocent body that must be made spectacular in a hotel room. Shirley is my name and I was born with a silver spoon in my toothless mouth. I was born to have certain parts of my body carefully wrapped in plastic. Louise Bourgeois made a model of me. Made spiders for me. I can't remember. Who has written all these sonnets?

But what a shining animal is man,
Who knows, when pain subsides, that is not that,
For worse than that must follow – yet can write
Music, can laugh, play tennis, even plan.

Edna St. Vincent Millay
SONETT CLXXI

Louise? Are you there? What's that? Humans who may no longer be human? Why are you running? Are you hunted? They hunt them as they were hunted, that's how it's written in the law, on the walls of the pigsty. What's that? Not a monster. It's a human being. Is she stuck in the 15TH night like the radiant angel?

We go our own ways, sometimes we meet, stop for a while, maybe we slaughter a part of ourselves in the sight of the other, offer a small part of our raw meat to each other, wrap our innermost names in fragile butcher paper, surrendering ourselves to each other in deep seriousness. Then the skin peeling begins. Is that the idea of literature? Is that what is called love? Animal army. King of milk. Street of thighs. Shot gun. I made it first!

NORRA SKOLGATAN

*No, my face the white face remains white in the white
ashes, the dead lover's face, the white in the white, my
face remains white as they devour my horse out there in
the white white powder...*

(The Evil Flower) Hepatica Nobilis

I cut lettuce. I cut off a finger. Have to throw away the salad. If only he hadn't stopped me.

bluebell
bluebell

It's easy to kill one another. The dealer lingers, a bag of chips in his hands, nodding off on the couch. *Please do not call the ambulance, let's die this time, we deserve to die this time.*

The dealer calls the ambulance. How many times are we supposed to be dragged across the sidewalk? How many times are our extra doses of Nalaxone supposed to last?

The ambulance staff bring us gifts for every visit they are forced to make to our apartment.

Our mutual shadow play with healthcare, the law and institutions is wonderful theater.

When my lover returns to life, I don't tell him that he's actually supposed to be dead but that I failed to kill him, and that I'm so sorry I failed.

I am so sorry.

I tried to keep the door shut when the ambulance woman came but she was stronger than me.

Why is everyone stronger than me when all I dream about is bodybuilding? She broke in and destroyed our death.

There's an intention behind everything I do, even though you never believed it.

We have friends over at dinner. I have murdered my lover. Am I to blame for getting blood all over the lettuce? For writing a confession from within the red flower.

The salad is in the trash, *the time is now.*

(He is not here anymore. So he forces me to play both victim and killer.)

I thought he would thank me. But he didn't.

Next time we will use coat hangers for our arms, baby.

I'm not going to ask my Greek choir for forgiveness or even permission.

I invite my audience to eat the bluebell salad and blood in the final hour.

I'm a pig oink oink.

Come my winged horse and heal me.

I'm burning his parents' house down.

I'm using a bluebell.

MAYBE THIS SILENCE WOULD BE MORE PEDAGOGICAL
IN A SLAUGHTERHOUSE

Heads or tails? The midwife tells me that locusts represent a form of masculine self-hatred – a masculine farce, an abject masculinity, a sickness – and that my spasms are not enough to incriminate our culture. Heads. I pick heads.

Tomorrow you will be forced to return to the language into which you were born. Your mother's crypt. Her sewage hole. The green riffraff, what a beautiful lady! Ha! You write like you want to smash a doll's porcelain head. You write the same way you put on make-up: with great precision, as if your life depended on it. Black and red. You move your arms as if there were locusts on them. That's how you write. The trashed posters still stand in for all that you have relinquished. Today let's write a swarm allegory about my heart. My heart and your shame.

Heads. I still pick heads.

This is the hiding place. Shirley's hovel. Her love, which has spread to Louise, has no aim but inevitably results in a swarm of emotion. With this swarm of emotion in something like the background, Louise makes art out of all her dead men.

Dear Honeypie

If everything is tip-top and you're happily married and so on, that's fine by me. But if you ask me, I think your partner is either in love with me or, more likely, absolutely dangerous. When violence is brought together with sex, you soon find yourself surrounded by men who are into such things, buzzing like fat flies around the sugar. It's a matter of time before mothers like you get black eyes ... You're still my sugar. When will we meet again? Preferably before I can die. The methadone dosage is now the highest. I don't have that long left.

I had to do it, I was your little sugar cube, you hated anyone who put their fingers in me, these are my sugar tracks, you're not alive enough to lick me, so I let others do that.

Somewhere in the quarantine, I can hear a woman sing "Your boy-
friend's back" and "He hit me and it felt like a kiss." I would hunt her
down, track her down, fill her mouth with bombazine, but I know that
she's the one who has a shotgun. She's the angel of the quarantine.

The Song of the Angel Made of Bombazine

Bluebell
Pegasus Pig
Dinner has already been contaminated
Hide under the table
Puke out the contaminated blood
Pour another glass of wine
Sing a drinking song
Bluebell Blues
Dirty Junkie Blues
You sing so beautifully
Your song is clean

SONGS FROM THE FUTURE

(One whore from Joyce, one from Fassbinder)

James Joyce's Whores

Picked a turkey hen clean? Easy come, easy go! That's what I said, wasn't it? Sweetness is sweet. The sweetness of sin. She is the bird who can sing but refuses to. It is said that a woman loses some of her charm with every piece of clothing she takes off. Ha! Don't forget to write back to me. I will write to you. How did we leave things? What did we do? She can't remember. The water is still running. The world will never be this quiet again. But there's room for debauchery. Take the bull by its horns. We've run into each other before. God knows where we've been? The second drink does it. Once is enough. He is certainly the best of them. He'll lose his money. What do you need? Promiscuous nudity often takes place around here, right? Yes! Rubber objects. Extra strong. Quality products. Will cure nervous disorders, otherwise money back guaranteed. Looks like you're a lively girl. Surely you are a lively girl? Her backbone is a bit slack. Married, I see? Should we go further or go back? Too difficult? Out with the tits. Happier now. Lower your shoulders. What is offered? Dressed to fetch and carry a basket in your mouth. Nice and deep! Well, boys? Do you have hard-ons now? Take a measure if you want! Must be a virgin. Clearly. Fresh breath. Clean. First, I'm going to test-drive her. Though she was not worth the price she asked for. On the other hand - who is? She's crazy. Wasted money. One eighty too much. Pretty scrawny. They pay by weight. You can borrow my fur coat, dear children. How weird that they liked her then? Even the best today. Eine meine mee, I'll fuck on your knees, eine meine muu, the hole is part of you. Best to talk first? Or just leave? I know I can go. I'll go if I want to. Have always done that. It grows in your stomach. The black water inside. The bottom cannot be seen. First-class breeding animal, one egg per hour. Up you go, my pearl! Maybe she is crazy? Hydrophobia. As a woman, she wants everything from behind. Stinks like a ferret. Hahaha. Uncertain movements. Nice dog! Fifi! Nice dog! Just do it then it's over. Are you writing to me? Down on all fours. My wife likes it in the mouth, swallows the last drop. An ocean of sperm. Does what she's best at. Rubber woman. Peephole Virgo. Does foreign trip mean loving a foreign woman? Yes, sir. Thank you, sir. No, sir. Yes, sir. The mouth full of geranium and peach. Vaseline. Lukewarm water. The foot is asleep. Will it be all night or just for a while? Are you hungry? Yes, aren't you? I have not eaten properly since lunch. So what do you want? Anything. Whatever there is. What is there? Now it's raining again. The dark water is spreading. The child's eyes are tearing up. Is the water a mirror? No. Rarely smoke, honey, didn't I tell you that? Just a cigar every now and then. She is in her own company now. Has always been. The smell of her lonely breath. Terror. Night Cream. Poppy. Anesthetic. Dream. In heat. Onion. Rotten. Sulfur. Classy. Desert. Infant. There is no truth. All that remains is faith in God and a desire to be turned inside-out by the righteous on Judgment Day. But they will never take her children. The child is the new world. The new animal. Does she dare to remember the night? On the bottom of the river. You are in the wrong place. Stop, I said! Beautiful paw. Should the baby be all night or just for a while? Who is the beast with two backs at night? Who sees himself in the lake? Who is a breeding animal? No one will touch her back. Is it really violence that she has been exposed to? In the wilderness only the cold-blooded can survive. She is cold-blooded, she is applause-blooded, she is crash-blooded. She decides what is and what is not violence. Is it a dragonfly or a drowning girl? No, do not touch her! She will always have her vertebrae and her teeth left, even when she is slack. Despite the rot. There's rustling in the trees. Lick your sword, protect the dark water fermenting in your stomach. Turn around. Lystra! There is a beautiful house facade in the countryside, there is ivy and a small chimney, there is a person on the other side of the water waiting for her, he seems to want to throw himself into the water for her and drift away ... Are you writing to me? Are you still here? Am I here?

MY MAKEUP HASN'T DRIED YET AND I'VE ALREADY WRIT-
TEN A POEM ABOUT EXPERIENCE.

The dog girl, Joyce virgin, Woolf daughter, wolfhound... Listen! Listen to how she speaks, she speaks so loudly and clearly! It's because she's the only one who can hear herself speak.

If you see the blue flower, ask it about distance. If you see my daughter, ask her why she is in so much pain. If you see a factory owner practicing child psychology, steal his daughter! The black garbage bag, will you put it over my head? Ask me where it hurts. Wait until the dog is beaten. Iowa. Funeral. A wreath of flowers. If you've already broken windows, you can laugh instead of cry, right? Laugh for the camera, turn on the radio. Listen! That crashing sound is coming from our catwalk. Listen!

Yes, I am my own mistress. I am the sustained tone. And you are scratches on the fabric. Wait to pee until you really need to pee, it gets so horribly dusty on the road when you pee. If you pee on a cat, it becomes a pissy kitty, if you miss, it becomes a miss kitty. The fabric that is woven during the day is scratched up during the night. Don't turn off the lamp! Curses, prophecies. Self-reflecting girl. No, you can't edit her. The most beautiful girls are the haunted girls. Didn't you know that? Then you must have missed something. Mom and Dad speak through me. They think I'm the fire. No one dares to call her by her real name. She's on fire. All stories live in the body. In her body. It's not my fault. We are all guilty of having created the gods.

Your words become her earth. She could be anyone. Whoever she wants to be. Care for the red girl. Water the red flower. She is the fire. No animal calls fire by its proper name. All animals find a hundred different ways to name the fire. They dare not get too close to her. They are afraid of the burns. They live in mortal fear of fire. She is our fire. She keeps the herd alive. Elsie! For our dead mother's sake! Damn it! What a wolf grin! Who found the yellow sunflower? Yes, it is certainly genuine! She gave birth to herself in a meadow. No, in a pile of stones! She is so sweet and kind. A real woman. With cute panties. Who poured honey and syrup down the underpants? But she poured her laughter over the world! It still echoes. No, it's not dangerous. She is not dangerous. Let her be. Don't stick your tongue out at her. Did she really wish for a more dangerous fauna? The Madonna has no eyes. She still gets everything when she ties her tongue. Do not try! Do you feel your tail wagging even though you no longer have one? Which German swear word is the most beautiful? She doesn't know that. She doesn't know German. Never knew German. Hahaha! It does not matter. Death metal. Enjoy, golden girl, enjoy. No, she's not a stalker. She doesn't need to follow anyone. Everyone follows her. You also. But didn't you hear what I said? You, too, are weak for this piece of sugar. She melts in your mouth. Swallow her whole. Do not worry. You won't burn yourself. You will not suffer from illness. Nor from the blood infection. The red flower. Flared the jaundice. Take her hand and she will follow you to the end of the world. It is very stupid to be complicated. She is Elsie. She has no roots. Not stuck anywhere.

Why does it have to be so dark in here? We make the world a summer meadow. Illuminates the world with the radiance from within. Sitting us down and peeing on a daisy. She is a girl. She is not sick. SHE IS NOT SICK. Her name is Elsie. She married The Lonely Wolf. Say, are you my Great Uncle? Wrap my feet, baby. Mummify me beautiful. I'm your eternal jewelry, right? The dress is creamy white and I have pastries tattooed on my butt. Have you seen? Her magical birthmark! You're cunning, you old cock. Do you want a kiss? Fast! Fast! Where is her divining rod? Away with all the jealous sissies. The girl has sent out her spies. Everything is true! And no one escapes. (sugar trace)

Stupor: I am drawn to the crimson girl. I cut her crimson flower. It's the fire flower. No animal calls the fire by its true name. All animals have hundreds of ways to name fire. They dare not come too close. They are afraid of her. The crimson girl with her paraphernalia. They live in fear of fire. She keeps the flock alive.

Why is it so dark in here? Why is it so cold? Why do you think I'm a prostitute? We should make the world into a summer meadow. Light up the world from inside. Sit down and pee on thousandbeauties. I'm your eternal piece of jewelry, right? The dress is cream-colored and I have cakes tattooed on my ass. Do you want a kiss? Quick! Quick! Before Louise ruins everything! Quick!

We're learning how to speak again because we're graduating. The world ends this week. The world began with ignorance and it will end with ignorance. Put a seed in your mouth. The dean of the congregation hammers my little nails. He tells us to close the gate that leads to the ivory tower. But who will teach me how to speak? Why does my mouth taste like blood? Bbbbblllllbbblblodschb? The meat clump grows in my belly. I feed the hares. I feed the whores. I mutter. I'm Mother Goose. Darling darling honey pie. Oh-fucking-phelia. You're my crazy Hamlet, my pathetic lover, dead since two months back. Rest in peace. I love you. I only recognize myself in you. I'm also carrying that which you carry. I can't find the right words to describe that. Every day I open the junk mail expecting to find your obituary. Don't disappoint me. Death, death metal, junk poet. I am still your stalker. Still ready for your funeral. Ready to blow up balloons, to throw lipstick-smeared cigarette butts on your grave. Ready to be Elsie for you.

This is the only quarantine where the dead come alive and the living die. That was the first and only lesson Louise gave me. Now when she is gone I have to remind myself of her words. Her rule is the only knowledge for survival in this asshole-crypt. And the only reading instruction that means anything to our audience.

There goes a person. There. He talks, laughs, gestures. He walks alone. He keeps walking. Perfect! What a prophet! All druggies are prophets in their own worlds! And I have been granted the gift of understanding prophets. I've heard so many prophesies I can't hear a word from a normal person anymore. The room is cold and naked. Take off your clothes. I said, Take off your damned clothes! Everyone goes to bed at 7 pm. Nobody's pardoned. There are no chairs to sit on. Everyone hick-ups and burps and spills. The toilets are smeared with shit. Who has stolen the paper? There is no toilet paper. What is he going to use to wipe himself with? Wipe your mouth. There are fluorescent lights in the ceiling. They are bright. Turn out the lights! Turn out the lights I said! Can't you hear? You can't keep any knives or scissors or even balls of yarn. The evening light hums. Louder than madness. Whoever claimed that madness would be our burden on this earth? Hey come here and I'll show you. There's virginity in there. Hey. Great stuff! Hey shit-pants, aren't you going to off yourself? Ha ha ha. What are you doing? Don't you have a soul? OK, wander around without a destination. Without a chain around your neck, dear stray dog, out in the wild. Those dogs die. The stench from his rotting body floods the city and brings disease and sickness but that's OK. Nobody can sleep anyway. It's not his fault. It's never been his fault. Slow down! Shirley has no roots, but she has white thighs and wags her tail. Who is panting inside of you? Is that Shirley?

END GIRL

THE VIRGIN STATE

You only see the flower from above. Everything is at a distance here. Even the hare bells. I learn that hare bells are sometimes called blue bells from Shirley, while we imagine things to do to each other's bodies. The twentieth night seems particularly hospital-like when we talk about flowers like this. She tells me Louise's symbol is the tortured lilac. She says my torso has the sweet smell of hare bells. I think I'm crying but I'm merely remembering a dream I once had. My lips hurt when I came to. Shirley reminds me that this is the kind of night that is meant for riots. She spits out the hare-seeds. She looks at my hairless chest. Hyena. When you're born in front of a camera, I suppose you never stop hating the flatness of bodies. I tell her about the dream. The shooting range, the smeared fruit.

If you see my daughter, ask her where it hurts. Take her away from the séance. The hospital party. The party on the ashes of my bedsheets. My childhood. My twentieth century of cut-out hearts. Ask her where she wants to go for her birthday. Ask her how much candy she can eat in one hour. Ask her what she thinks about blue bells. You don't have a daughter.

YOU CAN ONLY HEAR THE IMPOSSIBLE VOICES
WHEN YOU BURN DOWN THE QUARANTINE

When I entered this quarantine I was still under the illusion that I was alive. That I could eat as much funeral candy as I wanted. That my teeth would rot and then my camera would break against a beautiful body. Was it your body, Louise? Do you own my body too? If you ask me where it hurts, I'll lie to your face. I'll say, in the blue bells. But I'll mean: Your body is beautiful. I mean to involve it in smuggling. Your beautiful body and its horrifying aftermath. Covered in bombazine.

I mean: turn on the radio. The electric sounds come from our catwalk. The spiders. The wreath of flowers. The crash-and-pony show. Our audition. The bite-mark on your thigh. The crash-and-burn party on Hymns for the Twenty-First Night. I'm learning to cry again from you, Shirley. I'm learning to look hot in front of the camera even when I'm cold. Stop! Freeze! I'm freezing. Snap. Don't kiss me when I'm this cold. I miss your kisses but I can keep the pitch. I will tear your skinblue fabric with nails from the underworld. The wonderworld: when I'm standing in it, I have no words for kiss or mouth. I'm in a crossed-out state. Don't kiss my face. Things are bad and getting worse on the road back to the mother tongue. The road is lined with corpses. The road is my catwalk. If you kiss a cat, it becomes a piss-cat; if you miss it will be a kiss-miss. The language that is spoken by day is garbled by Louise. At night, in the dazzling chamber of the quarantine where photographs of the disaster line the wall, poetry makes mouths happen.

BOMBS MAKE BODIES HAPPEN INSIDE THE NEW QUARANTINE

Poetry makes night happen in my mouth. My whore mouth, which is full of hare bells. Poisonous. Louise laughs. She has a gross little snake for a heart, and the stained pelt is her butterfly.

NIGHT #22

NIGHT #23

I've heard it's hygienic to write elegies. The blue flower is a good omen. If you see it during an accident, you will survive impact. Translation. You will speak a mother's tongue in order to stay intact. In order to keep the child alive. Shirley tells me she's explaining to Louise, her violence as the most toxic state. Translation. I'm intact when I see my daughter in my toxic dream and she asks me if I'm her dad. No, not intact. There's a different economics at play. I speak the father tongue to her: I lie. Translation. I tell her she's my daughter and I'm her father. It's me, your father. Translation. I'm buried in debt. Because of her. I still write poetry. An inflationary economics: This is how I father. But I'm also like Louise, I smell like rotten lilacs on account of art. Translation. Art has no Father.

ART IS THE FATHER, TRANSLATION THE CORRUPTION

To walk through these gates, I tell myself, means to walk into someone else's language. Meaning bioaccumulates, I relate to Shirley. Radium imitates calcium to the point of being incorporated into the human bone. The human bone: If I'm going to pay for it, I'll have to talk to Louise. With spiders crawling all over the orchard. In Louise's spider there is a hole. I put my pinkie in it. It puts its pinkie in me. I finally learn how to speak. I say *more, more*. I say *more, more*. I learn to giggle. The giggle of black flora. Louise is angry. This ridiculous song will force her to abandon the quarantine and take her father-violence out into the world. And I live out there. In the toxic world. With my father-body and the halfway marvelous corpse of a butterfly in which art bioaccumulates. The barium-colored thing has begun to flutter again. The funeral has begun to sound out the alarms again. The emergency state, the crash: I've experienced all of these states. The state I have yet to enter is the virgin state. I will cut it.

Someone has carved a little wooden horse. The artist smuggles it out. The father sells it to me. I'm a foreigner so I need some memories, a childhood, to replace the one that infects the quarantine. Children are contagious, memories of childhood even worse. Sara Tuss has brought a new wig for you, Shirley, to wear when you stand by the large window and you are chilly even though it's spring. Then you're Louise. I can tell from the photograph of the riot that you belong to violence when you are this happy. This crossed out. I've been crossed out too and the joy it gave me was frightening. The voice I speak in is violence, sound, counterfeits. It will not help me escape and it will not help Sara Tuss find her childhood. In my memory of your childhood, your love has to destroy. You want to understand last night as a form of hygiene. Now you're ultrapure.

The guiding principle of the quarantine is that it hurts to be ultrapure. The window hurts when one's arm goes through it. My arm goes through it in a work of art. My face goes ultrapure: it's the state in which I belong. Virginity: you can only reclaim it though violence. The guiding principle: You have to leave this state. You will no longer need to freeze. In horror, you will realize that you have no further father to incriminate. You will stand by the large window in the wig I have bought for you, Shirley. You will go for acetylene.

I go for contamination. I go for chemistry. Art as volatility. This voice belongs to imperialism. New Jerusalem. This voice has to warn me about sound, what it does to meaning, what it does to sex. The narrator's name is written in cursive in a letter from Louise. Or a man who is under Louise's spell. Louise or the attractive man under her spell tells the narrator to invent her father from the wreckage. It's glassy and brittle, the wreckage. It's a poor electrical conductor. Louise tells the narrator to rewrite the potent chemistry of the prostitutes and their acetylene beauty. They are virgins in the new version. The war version, the snow version, the version with all the angels and smeared berries. In the cold version, Sara Tuss asks Louise about several factors pertaining to the prostitution angle, including the presence of light and certain catalysts that can facilitate the rate of decomposition. Louise asks her about her own experiences with prostitution. With art. How can you be so beautiful in such cheap hotel rooms? How can you be so soiled? She asks about the spoons that used to cover her body. They glowed like they were made of cold silver, Sara remembers. Louise asks her if she is Elsie or Shirley. She doesn't know yet who she is in the room. She puts the silver spoon in her mouth and enacts a crash. She drinks vinegar and eats chalk. She runs through the corridors carrying a locked box of rotting apples. She wants to be me, the virgin and the liar.

It's dangerous to leave the quarantine! Do you think you can fool me? No wigs in the world can keep you from your grief. We came here together, we'll leave together. Or not at all! Sixteen more nights in this underworld!

The father who steals your novel: His horse is sweet, poisoned. You want to ride it in the Victorian era. Your symptoms include muscle weakness and skin rashes. What remains is to live under his name (Mercury). To walk through the gates he has dedicated like something out of science fiction to the umbilical cord. You know what he means: He wants to celebrate belonging. You want to celebrate morphine. You always thought the figures around the gate were hyenas but they look intricated with lanceolate leaves which are aromatic when crushed. Mercury-poisoning is a risk. You're protected by a man but you have the attributes of cutting plants. You are accomplished by seeds. You have schneeflocke fluttering like serious insects in your pink seam. You have no narrative arc. The gates look more beautiful when you're high: The hyenas have a cool, silvery-blue-green cast. The leaves have approximately 7 lobes that are dentate or sinuate, and the leaf base is cordate. The plume poppies have creamy white apetalous flowers. Your innermost name is written in rotten hydrangeas. Since my name is written on a mound of dirt, my novel will always be transformed by your drugged-out voice, your hydrangean voice.

YOUR HYDRANGEAN VOICE COMES INSIDE MY MOUTH

What am I going to do with my own wreckage when I'm lost in your quarantine, dad? What am I going to do with my own slab of raw meat? How can I log out? I can't. I make an imposing display: coral bells, spiked speedwell, cushion spurge, white snakeroot. I press them in the pages of your delicate novel about my lips.

OINK OINK WHO'S THERE

Your name is entirely or largely obliterated by the progress of spring. Because you want me to poison you, hemlock you, you are now Louise. Louise carries fleeceflowers to my hospital room in order to dominate my aura. I have a sage aura. I have a choke aura. A floral aura. An aura that has to be answered. Louise can only survive sub rosa. Needlelike, Louise wants to corrupt my childhood memories with her shellpink language. It's a language for stalking. She is stalking me with earlier flowers in her hands, which smell like gasoline. Louise wants every notched corolla lobe of the meadow to penetrate my cold poem about silk, my thighs, morphine. Inside your beautiful hotel room, you want to dream the foliage into words. Louise dreams of a comatose-textured place where I can't be forgiven. It's also the room in which you were made into a spoon language. Art's cut language: you want it to speak to you like silver. Want it to come out of you like a mockery of virginity. Like a worm. You want to shell out for my torso. Your money means paradise in postcards from my hometown. You can have the entire bestiary for free. Nature is a Heraclitean Fire.

It is not enough to study the life of a single star, Shirley. Depending on the mass of the star, its lifetime can range from a few million years to trillions of years. You are Shirley now because you speak like this now. Like a star. Flaunting forth your glitter throngs. The stellar changes are happening gradually to your whitedazzling body inside the crypt. I'm in the crypt with you but not for a trillion years. I will be King Bloom because the spasms in my right arm lead to inflorescence consisting of a cyme with four to six flowers. In this boisterous crypt Louise has handled your spherical shell while wearing a red wool dress with a lozenge twill pattern. The exocarp is pale, yellowish. The complex wood carvings are done in a gripping beast style. Inside the crypt, Louise carries the fruit in a wooden box, which contains the skeletal remains of fourteen horses and several dried stalks. I have ridden the fourteen horses and called them toxic. Louise has covered them with tarp. Louise has lined up sculptures along the wall. *That one is you when you have broken glass,* she tells me. You can't tell me which one I am because I'm not a replicant. The threadlike chain that is unspooling from the crypt has a fatal flaw in it. Fatal for Arachne. Her web has a hole in it. It causes spasms. She can't breathe. I'm Shirley and you are a girl with a spoon. What is this thing I want to do with the sun? Translation has to do with death. It happens in the underworld.

You are lost inside your own quarantine.
Every deed has to be accounted for.
Every drug transforms the star with which you bleed.
Drown the nation, dazzle your blackouts
for a trillion years. Do the Louise.

You do a biological Louise as if you were being paid trillions. I keep building tableaus to understand our translations in terms of texture and toxicity levels. I forgot to mention history to you when you wore that glass face, the one I cannot break. I wore the glass photograph in my mouth. You tried to prod it out of me. You said, History. I said, you've become Shirley's worst nemesis, the interrogator. We were violent with our bruises and our stained shirts. The things Louise has done in Casablanca we must do to each other while carrying each other through the quarantine you revealed to me. You wore a dress made of black lamb on your body. *Do the Louise*, you said. Everyone inside the crypt listened. *Do the Louise*, you said. I deserved to lie on glass. *I deserve to be handled like glass*, you said. In the henbane dream about glass bursting beneath my feet, you make holes in the quarantine. With your fingers. You're trying to enter my glass because it is soft now. I'm soft when I do the Louise. I do the Ash Louise, the Lash Louise for you. For you. For you.

FOR MY DEAD LOVER

Hi neighbor.

Hi God.

Your Cuban cigars.

The smoke you breathe into my face

while humming along to Public Enemy.

Your expressionist paintings.

All the code words I'm supposed to understand.

But I've never understood your garish paintings.

Your beautiful hand.

You beautiful hand that fists me.

I understand your hand.

Your junked body.

Your junked body that embraces me.

I understand your body.

Your stolen ties.

Your stolen ties tied around my arms.

I understand those ties.

Your new teeth.

You show off your new teeth and you look beautiful.

You will take those beautiful teeth with you into the grave.

You won't leave me a single tooth.

I have knocked on your door for 35 days and 35 nights

but you haven't opened.

For whom would you open the door?

I sit down outside your door and weep.

I can smell us.

We smell sour and milky like flowers.

Lily of the Valley.

Liljekonvalj

You will never open this door for me again.

Did we ever exist if I am the only one left to remember us?

When you were still alive you helped me carry the memory of us.

And now?

What did you think.

Are you going to open this door?

Are you going to open me up?
Tear the spider web out of us?
Will you stay there?
You live deep inside the crypt.
Behind your ribs a spider has spun her web.
It protects you but
the poison kills you.
I long for a memorial.
I long for us together in the street.

I am nobody without you.

I have been aging for a long time now without you.

You never got to see my aged face.

I never got to see your aged face.

I wanted you to see my wrinkles.

I wanted you to see my child.

I wanted to give birth to your child, but I never told you that, I thought there would be time for that, in a sober future, when we would have gotten rid of all the bottles, when we would have burnt away the black sun from our devour-hole, the devour-howl. When we would have wished ourselves gone. When we would have rubbed the red from our eyes. When we would have been liberated from soft powder that was scattered over us. Petrify our mourning robes.

I talk to you at night, quietly, so that nobody will hear me. So that my child won't hear me. So that my husband won't hear me. So that my sobriety won't hear me.

Every night is a night of tears.

I don't know how to do this.

I don't know how to continue.

Don't know how this will end.

Who am I now?

I can't stand you.

I've never been able to stand you.

I can't stand myself without you.

Everything is plague and cholera.

I can't unhear your prophesies.

A POEM ABOUT HYGIENE AND
A POEM ABOUT EROTICS

First Poem

In the barn I think
I'm at the house for labor pains
(that's the name of the animal)
but no animal will escape from me again
my monster is a sow
I suckle her

I drowned the cackling chicken in gasoline
the historical adventure novel for women
bubonic plague pneumonic plague
black rat *(rattus rattus)*
bury your victim
in my stall

Rats dance naked
my petticoat is warmed
I can't live together
with this haunting
I also can't
live without it

The one who learned the lyrics is the one who can sing, but when no one sings there's silence. The silent roles frighten the children. I shut up when Shirley least expects it. Save the fur, sharpen the claws. What should I say about her behind her back, when she's no longer here, long after she has disappeared? She's not going to listen. She has her own head to listen to. Huh, what did you say? Do not you trust me.? I'm primitive and without wings. Our mass medium is at maximum volume. I'm the best show this den. My thoughts are survivors of a terrorist attack. I am kinder than my mother. Bigger and tastier. She is not going to call herself the violent or ungrateful child anymore. She's going to be taking over the world now. Born to be heir to the throne. Huh? A bird hatched an egg and the girl misplaced herself. Did she get caught in the net? No! No longer. What? Both sides of the same coin. No more up and no more down. No more hesitation. The world rests on her shoulders.

But little mom, go to bed, it's still night. The night is mine. I'll take over. No! Wait until the time is right. Don't get ahead of events. Everyone is welcome, even those who cheat on her. Bitch! Clap your hands! Wait for the river. Wait! Clap your hands until they turn tomato red. Do you love when my hair stands up straight? Now I sleep in a very old city. In a small caravan. The world is so small so small. Don't be afraid of the hole in my face, it's far too small for you to fit in it. Have! Roots should always be left behind. If you take them with you, you turn into living death. She is not a living dead. The demon carries no burden. She is the new queen of air. She is a swamp girl. Drink her scald. She shouldn't have her hair done. Nor shall the she-wolf tear her clothes. The world belongs to her. The words too. Not that they would be included in her dictionary. She sucks at words. She is spring. She lashes out. Wince! She chops the leg. Rabies rohypnol. Mouth full. Start over. Domna mother. Take over. Limit the brother. This is not a peeping toy. She is not your mummy doll. Bbbbblllllllbbblblodschb? Has she never been. Oh mom, so you drag me. Oh mom, the broth is boiling over! Oh mother, leave me alone! Mom, haven't I done everything for you! In fact, there is no evidence of any dirty deeds on my part. None at all! Where is the boss now? Here! Here she has always been. (sugar trace)

My face is worn out from the nights
I still haven't survived
my face is a den of bulls
my face
rattledout

This must be the rat face I got
when I moved in
to my brother's living room

I have lost
the postcard collection from my hometown
the study of the pests that infested our lives
but I was still too young to remember
  the abyss

I suffered through the ordeal
while going to class
where I studied the law   I thought
it would help me
silence the barn   I thought
it would corrode my face   I thought
it would help me burn up the animals
and make a necklace from horse's teeth

Still, there's no rattling in her!

Instead, she paints sentimental landscapes
and transforms herself into a children's choir

Don't take my word for it

Touch my lips with your favorite shard from the dirtiest glass

She faces the kind of act whose meaning and purpose is constantly changing; she finds a burnt spoon, she finds a nail. This is the inside of this poem. This attic. It is the grave of this poem. She finds a hair tie, a lipstick, a cheap plastic comb. She finds disparate parts to make mouths with. She measures the cut that runs right through the kingdom.

Second Poem

Those experts have never tickled a baby
with a crochet hook. They don't even know how hungry
I am
or why my Jerusalem is as fragile as a rib

We made love. That's the only thing we did. Isn't that true? And demanded. A distant world. To be so close. Are you trembling little child? Cracks widen. The streaks of you are the recurring variety. You. A rough memory: You, like a scar, surrounded by a ravaged landscape, all the trees chopped down. You're a blank spot on the map, no feelings. Therefore I can swallow pearl necklaces. The dark is impenetrable. By repeating the past we are transforming it. Your presence is as imaginary as the present!

My face
I live outside my own self-reflecting colony

Maybe you have heard about the oldest city
the one mentioned in The Bible
in the first book of Moses

That city is still guarded

If you want to get rid of me you're out of luck
I've tried my whole life
We have to be twins with the same goal
annihilate us

We have to be a cold war
 a moist and sloppy little war
Neither of us will win until we've been
exposed in tabloids, until we've swallowed the pills
Unfortunately neither of us are sentimental enough
to put out cigarettes on each other's arms
We were born with doves in our mouths
their beaks are our genitals
as the barnyard
full of merciless animals who are trying to escape
come out to play
Come out to destroy our wedding
My girlfriend will not acknowledge
the animals
She's an expert

This pain –
Will it ever end
I thought I had buried the child.
You have no child.
Invite more friends to the party por favor.

THE STORY OF THE
BRIGHTGREEN ANGEL

(The Unreachable Place)

- What's that?
- Another kind of girl, a bird-like predator with radiant wings,
a skull of nuclear reactionary brilliance, the opposite of the
green, green instead evil, green let it stay green, scared green
even though the colors are not visible in the ether

Sure, you could say that you once knew a girl who wanted to be an angel but since she wasn't an angel and probably would never become an angel she was just a girl and to become an angel she had to die. We are the ones who transform the girl into an angel. We turned her into a simple porcelain object. We did that to her. She was no terminator. She was no predator. Girls don't just become angels. Death is just as flat and meaningless as life. Nobody can transform into angels or predators except the centerfold girl with goose-feathers on her back, bunny ears on her head and white lace on her body. Life goes on. The noose is brought down but nobody forgets the dangling body. Life goes on. Everything else becomes angelic. The one who comes back to watch over the ones left behind is not an angel. She's rotten meat, bones, burnt-up hair, ashes. She's all of that, but no angel. She's no angel.

You can't even remember her real name, but she's no salt statue or Eurydice petrified in the underworld, no angel. Literature tells us that she became an angel, but literature lies. That's the first pillar of literature: literature lies. It's a palace of lies, a sorrow play. Don't trust a single word in this quarantine. I've tried to flee from language in order to become radiant, but where did the light come from again? Was it the mouth or the anus? Or from your fly?

We barely made it out of the city
before transgressive nature
pulled out the plug
You're probably rolling your eyes
You probably think I should have grown out of
the role of the failed king
in a farce I still imagine feels shocking
for everyone but me
I am the one that's stuck
Nobody is shocked
not even the dead

I'm rolling my eyes.
Nobody feels shocked
Not even my dead lovers
The role of Louise
is unfinished
because it belongs to me

A radiant ghost (brightgreen mother figure because even dead mothers are bright green) sits there dead and unreachable, peeling a rotten orange while reading out loud a few lines from Bataille that I hadn't read before: Everyone knows it feels good to cry, that one finds in tears a kind of consolation one doesn't actually want to accept but which overwhelms.

Our time inside the quarantine is almost up.

When I was small, my parents gave me a gun to keep me from crying.

It wasn't loaded. Was it, Shirley?

That was yesterday.

Tomorrow I give my daughter her name.

It's Gun.

Oh so you're in this poem now

You with your fingers and curls and
the mayhem you always manage to confuse with intimacy
If it's a ghost town you want out of life
find a man of feathers
or a saint from The Great Polio Epidemic
If it's siege you want, penetrate me
then throw me back to the hole

My favorite product comes from translation

The elevator at the top of the high-rise of testimonies

My collapse is the ground zero of literature

My favorite phrase is a raised fist from the riots

My favorite commercial is the swimming pool that swallowed my brother

Everything is devoured by chlorine, oblivion

Are you still my love

Have you chewed up your own face

The fiction goes to my head

Fiction is the most horrifying jaw of reality

Drool for me

Fighting animal

Nightstyle

Crush the tablets and inject them with IV

That's my best tip

Die.

It's a bit like a coloring book
for children with attention deficit
disorder a bit like annihilating
a civil war with a civil war

baby mother

Once she was a very young and promising authoress
I wrote without limits my way out of my own psyche
I had no sense and no sense of decorum
all these small creatures with sharp teeth and stinking mouths
they were very sexy
locked up in their own forest
stuck in the portal

What happened to the promising writer
was she even promising and
has she ever been young
now she laughs it off

I'm eternally grateful
that my fucked-up parents had not expectations for me
other than the assumption that I would be a fuck-up
that makes me laugh now
but I never found my own laughter
and now I'm a wandering spirit lost in my own text
and here I will remain stuck
until the next book
and the next book
which will never be written
because the laughter is so loud

baby mother is ready for slaughter
for forty nights she shall be slaughtered
the unwritten novels are burned at the stake
mutations warp in blue flames

whose civil war is being staged
who is in charge of the film crew
is it always louise who pulls the strings
the queen without a mouth cavity

Don't paint over the paintings I worked so hard on. You've never under-stood my sacrifices. I've never understood your fingers. How they move like mayflies. You've always confused me with your sense of intimacy, your naked body, that mayhem that blurs the line between your appear-ance and what you are trying to tell me in a film. You're trying to tell me about your past but you're plagiarizing the lines from a great film. I'm looking at you as though you were a saint from the epidemic. If it's a siege you want, penetrate me then throw me back in the hole. The ghost town. Slash open your pillows and cover me with feathers. Oh, so I'm in this poem now. Me and my favorite product. I'm translating your collapse as ground zero for literature. I'm locking myself up in the tallest tower. The watchtower: I can hear your music from here. I can see your body from here. My favorite part is your fist. The one I hate the most is my own fists. They're bleeding. I'm back home. I want to be devoured by a swimming pool. Are you still my darling? The fiction is getting to me.

Today's Radio Play

We sit opposite each other in a darkened room, between us the table top, we share an orange, she whispers: Stop using me for your own needs. Me: I need you, I need your look at me, I need your counterarguments. She: But I'm dead. Me: That's why I need you even more. She: To constantly reformulate your narratives, to constantly blur the edges, to constantly conduct self-criticisms that go beyond me and the memory of me and my dead body and my remaining sons and daughters? Make a decision sometime. Your fear of being independent is laughable. She: They have a language. She: You have that too. You write. But you didn't get the language as a gift from your parents, you got it as their curse. You continue to sketch out that state of ignorance, languagelessness. Me: You got more pompous towards the end. She: It was necessary to close the doors around me in order to undergo the final transformation. Me: That's not a transformation. That thing is dead. Just dead. She: Stop reading the codes so manically. They are merely reproductions, a constant, exhausting search for effects. Stick to your own codes instead. Me: I forgot my own codes.

How do I log out?

Shirley, the fiction will devour you.

Sick puppy. I advice crushing the pills and injecting them.

Smoke the Fentanyl. Die.

Shirley: My gun and I are the only ones keeping the family traditions alive.

Louise: Shirley, this is no time for a confessional poem.

Shirley: This isn't a confessional poem, it's a family history.

Louise: We're at the end of my family.

Shirley: You're the daughter of a million loose screws.

Louise: And you're the son of the century. The fortune son of the quarantine.

Louise: Shirley, stop doing that thing with my mouth.

Louise: We're a glamorous couple. Imagine us as a misreading of each other's shadow.

Johannes: You think they are doves, that they represent peace but I know that they represent my counterfeit heart.

Sara Tuss: I don't understand this place. Why are you trying to tear down this space we have built together.

Johannes: Do you want to be Shirley for a little longer? I can be whore-Louise and you can be chatter-Shirley.

Louise: Or I can teach you how to draw spiders with charcoal smudged on your hands and on your lips.

Shirley: I can feed you fresh strawberries because I'm back home now.

The Angel: Now you know my secret, my rifle, my role in the quarantine.

I've barely even touched my rifle. You've barely touched my rifle. You've scraped a word on the barrel or maybe it's the spiders. Instead of firing my rifle into crowds I've spend my nights reading my favorite book. It's a book of words. A dog has bitten the cover. It's a book of god and a bite of god. Rabies. Are there dog bites in your favorite book? Does your god have a jaw bone? Where is the light coming from? Narcotic, nuclear-green light from the angel buried in nature? That's my mother too. Eurydice has cut her own head off with her daughter's toy knife. Another way of putting that would be to say something quickly in a foreign language. Detta är det andra sättet. Jag vet inte hur man laddar ett sånt här gevär. I'm Shirley now. The other Shirley. The one who played Black Dahlia.

You need to have more pathos when you are Shirley. Have you already forgotten her bruised hips? Her love of the fist? I think about your skin a lot. What was it she wrote, Mayröcker? *I actually only have one internal language. It bubbles beneath the skin, horrified.* I brought Shirley to the factory but the owner wasn't there. She wanted to have children and a house with a pool, a library with beautiful books. She taught me how to be a man. I wanted to her to harm me. She was pleased. That's what being a man is. She finally had her man. I went home. That's how most games end. Most songs are ridiculous. Most empires are incestuous. I've sat next to this damned radio for hours now wanting to hear Shirley's voice but I can't make it out in the noise. Everything is your voice. You're inviting me into our end. The End. You want me to go in there with you. To play The End with you. To play The End with your horrifying paraphernalia. I'm doing it, I'm doing it. I'm bringing the rifle. The quarantine is almost over.

THE ANTENNA SHADOW

THE JUNK POET: First lesson: pomegranates are a poet's food.

SHIRLEY: Huh? And you are a poet?

THE JUNK POET: I live in a sandbox with cat piss and plastic toys and used diapers. Sure, I have access to an apartment in the Rose Garden, but that apartment is also used by other opium-smoking poets, if they're not now locked up in prison, you never know for sure. I prefer the sandbox to the prison. It is important to escape those who hunt you, it is important to avoid those like you, who want to steal my blood and smoke. It's hard to be a poet. To be and remain a poet means to never avoid describing the hunt. It is the only real thing, which I dare to assure you with a clear conscience. It is best done sitting on a horse. Ride ride creeper. With cloak and knight's gear. Who can see us getting used to it? Off and on, off and on. Spoken poetry has a much greater impact than written poetry. No! Quiet, say nothing, no objections. You should just keep quiet. Something is coming. Then it pours out all kinds of desecrations against everything holy and reasonable. I'm used to people like you. Flows of invention. These rivers the Harlot herself must float in. The flowing touch will bring Brutus himself back to life. Who is Brutus? Me of course! Who did you think? Don't stand there twiddling your fingers and glaring. You must be faster! Yes? What in this wide world could Brutus possibly object to after the Scrooge's latest finds? You rule in areas where you are not operating at the moment. Do you have any influence on my heart at all? I have no heart. How to break the heart of someone who has no heart? My betrayal is rooted in openness and honesty and insight. Where do you find openness, honesty and insight if not in the shards of a broken heart? Where can you not find prostitution if not in Skökan? Does the Whore have a heart?

SHIRLEY: It's pounding in my chest anyway.

THE JUNK POET: It always throbs in the little prostitutes, it's because they're so handy at hitting the curb. The first lesson is over. I will have even stronger stuff at home tomorrow.

SHIRLEY: I always come back to you.

THE YOUNG POET: Look, go.

SHIRLEY: Can't I stay? Just last night? Just a single night?

THE JUNK POET: Goodbye. See you. Dry the tears. My sandbox is open for you tomorrow, just like my heart and my flaccid cock. But now you have to leave me alone. I need to think. I have to say the poems out loud to my audience, to the cats, the plastic toys and the forgotten children. You don't belong to that crowd. Not yet.

THE CIRCUS PIG

Shirley has never seen her own backside. Shirley's void is our bliss of terror and tits. Shirley's back is a horse's back. No! Shirley's back is a camel's back. Place yourself between the humps. Shirley carries you through the desert landscape on her humpback. Shirley has no knowledge of her own strength yet. Shirley doesn't know she's transporting women with eight legs across the desert landscape. Should our sandbox represent death? There are no questions that Shirley asks herself. It is only us who ask ourselves such questions. Little does Shirley know that she is known for her own blood-thinning properties. Shirley has poked her own sphere. Shirley does not know the thin membrane that makes her impenetrable. Shirley doesn't know her own made-up face. Shirley has yet to come to grips with her own glorious backside. Shirley doesn't know she's our emotional freak. Shirley is the day that brightens our night. Shirley helps us in our fear of the night. Shirley is the woman who makes our night light, but she can't bear to be bright anymore.

The strained voice. Nothing is allowed to live here. Nothing alive. Not her. Nothing tender. Nothing green. Get down in the green now, Shirley. Put on a robe bred by a mother. Dress up in Louise's grief. The white goo sure dresses your face. Wrap yourself in the cloak of mourning. Your back is still covered in dark velvet. What are you hiding in your fat stores? You can't escape your own rear. Sad sad animals.

Did you meet the Junk Poet in his kingdom, Shirley? He calls his syringe "smoke" because he thinks it sounds more enchanting. He's a poet. It's in his nature to beautify. He has to beautify because he has never lived. You know how it works, Shirley, you who's such a talented actress. You have to enter into the sand to hide Louise's axe. You have found her hidden desert landscape, the sphere made from shattered glass. Milk yourself. You have the kind of fat that will last you all the way into death. Devour yourself.

I want you to bury that axe in my own back, in my own poem, in your back
(Louise)

I can't eat any more of our poems. The taste of poetry makes me sick. (Louise)

Log us out.
Night will soon turn to day.

It hurts Louise that she is constantly forced into personifying abstract concepts, such as death, love and puberty. Would be tiring for anyone, including Shirley, even though Shirley is used to disguises. Louise has dug her own ditch. Dug her own bed. Dug a whole out of history. It's up to Shirley to trip and fall into it. Let's leave Shirley's body inside the allegory. It's humiliating for her, but it's worse for the allegory. Horny bodies make allegories both so obvious and so impossible to bring into one's lives. It's the thirtieth night.

Do you interpret her body so that it fits the question at hand?

Do you interpret her body so that the actual message emerges?

Do you see her axe, how nicely it fits in her back?

Do you interpret her back?

Stockholm syndrome is the perfect blood disease for you.
Which quarantine are you stuck in? You who bury your wife in the floor of your luxurious floor? Your chamber drama is a stinking nail biter. You are related to the poet who was born in a sandbox. Your desert landscape is a castle at the best address in London. Bury me under the mink fur, tape me there, lick my arm crease if the needle gets stuck.

I've always dreamed of a man like you, a man with a hump of money that never ends, a man with a Danish storyteller in his name, a man with grief like a cloak to wrap me in, a man who already tasted his own downfall.

She, too, is a secret junkie queen behind the green mother mask, under the black cloak of mourning. Her blood-spattered flip-flops were left behind in the desert. The Junk Poet uses them as a pillow in the sandbox.

Quarantine is a pile of sand, a small Greek island in the sea of my forgotten dresses, in the sand melted flowers of blood. What's left in the closet? An opportunity to continue to rest in his own dumbness and his own ax blood. What's left in the closet? A chance to continue to lie in a broken deckchair and be fed with a silver spoon. What's left in the closet? The prospect of no longer having to express oneself, explain oneself, multiply oneself. Plastic bubbles. Defend yourself against the intruder. What's left in the closet? Pig literature.

SHIPWRECKED

I hid silver garments in the tree, but its metallic glow showed through the bark, now I want my scaly fish dress back. In the shade of the palm trees, my wounds are revealed. The drink tastes sour. Where is the moment her mother was impregnated by Gary Cooper's spirit? Who shoves half a lemon in their lover's face? Probably you, Johannes. I can help because I think lemon stings so nicely in the eyes, especially when the acidic liquid bursts the blood circulation. Do you often play with dead birds, Johannes? Poke feathers into the folds of your arms? Are you bright as a peony? Slip once more on the frozen blood congealed in the sand, that is, in your country's school yard. We are in need of it. In your new nation, your eyes were taped wide open, then you yourself closed them. There were too many corpses on the land. When we opened the bodies, we found no gold, only poisoned rain, unshed tears. In the European genocides, they took our fur coats at the door. Anyone who has to wash slime and blood off the floor of a ship is more likely to write an instruction book on how to collect dolls than how to write a poem. We've created a cold and very sticky doll in this tree. Well, it's still me up here, unlike before, when I was wearing a different mask. Until now, I haven't been ready to jump down on your sister's windowsill and sing her a sweet tune about loins, fire and terror. The smell of the coal, the heat of the gin. I put on the mask of betrayal. It itches.

Give me the crack junkies with clay feet

Give me the tarpaulin to hide the sailors

Give me the key to lock the closet

Give me gnostic dolls

Give me a doorknob to the poet's apartment

Give me the catatonic people who covers our TV eyes

Give me Louise as a grandmother

Give me Shirley as a daughter

Give me the rusty blanket

Give me the archetypes of sand

Give me the flour that grinds in my teeth

Give me broken teeth

Give me the picture that's still burning

Give me broken humps

Give me the underworld without cavities

Give me bragging rights and bragging rights

Give me the swollen shame of crowds

Give me proof of tampering

Give me desert empires

Give me a rapture of feathers and fire

Give me traces of laughter

Give me tigers

Elsie

My green mother's name is Elsie
Her name is the name of the syringe
I pushed into your arms

Elsie
Elsie
Elsie
Elise

si, yes
sil, yes

Target, the sharpest arrow, little sloppy syringe
What is your mother's name?
Your ex-girlfriend's name is Elsie
the sharp-eyed woman
Mother is standing in the wardrobe
and beckons you
casting his cobweb
and criticizes those who have lost their children
to the underworld

Shirley and Louise fight over Elsie

Elsie
Elsie
Elsie
Elise

Who plays the role of Elsie? The ex-girlfriend or the syringe-mother?
Can she be found in the closet? Do you have enough junk in your
breasts? Do you have enough squeal in your tits?

Elsie here's your shadow Elsie here's your seal Elsie here's your backside
Elsie it's stuck in the milk bowl Elsie you and your puncture wounds
Elsie your little indie band sucks Elsie I suck your tits Elsie I puncture
your balloon Elsie you're my milk sister Elsie my little surgeon Elsie my
tied up deer Elsie my solved problem in an abandoned vehicle

Turn off the lights.

What's left in the closet?

A Hollywood graveyard of dead horses. A torn instruction manual. A
castle of burnt silver spoons. A woman who did not survive.

Pig literature! Even though the island in the wardrobe is incredibly
Greek. Despite Shirley Temple dressing up as Calypso. Although Louise Bourgeois has watched too many TV shows. Despite the fact that
the ancient drama takes place in the closet. Arachne has cast her net.

YOU ARE PART OF THE NATURE THAT NEEDS CUTTING

THE EXPANSION OF THE CLONES

THE IMITATION OF HER DEAD ANATOMY
POISONED RAIN
THE FLOWERS IN THE SAND
WITH INTENT TO KILL
THE DEAD BABY IS STILL OUR ICON

I DON'T WANT TO SAVE ANY MORE SEEDS
FROM LOUISE'S THROAT

JOHANNES I CAN'T KEEP NEITHER WHISPERING
OR GROWING ANYMORE

JOHANNES WE HAVE NO OTHER CHOICE
MY WHISPERS HAVE TURNED INTO POOL WATER
CAN YOU EXPLAIN MY SALIVA?
CAN YOU SEE MY SEEDS?

HOW MANY LEGS DOES THE WOMAN HAVE?

Matter (Radio Play)

Shirley (whispering): I have been in nothingness but that experience is written off by the sculptresse (read Louise). I have to write about it on the back of her sculptures now. The words behind the shapes transform them into a bed, a thorn, the purged and apocryphal tools of my trade. Do not worry. My stowed-away soul must under no circumstances become visible. It has already burned in the fire. It has suffered burns. My charred little spirit. No one shall see the mutilation of my soul, other than as small diminutive holograms.

Who tunes the voice inside me?

Have you deluded yourselves, imagining that Shirley is the light of the night and I am the darkness of the day? Yes, you have deceived yourselves. Don't you understand that it has been the other way around? All along, it has been the other way around. (Louise)

The romanticized criminality suits literature extremely well, you don't have to see what is actually going on. Words can make everything feel tolerable. I accidentally fed my cat drugs. I am on trial at the social services office. I can't help it. I must remain in my first mind and the realm it keeps tricking me to join. (Louise)

Stop giving me traits and thoughts I've never had. I'm not malleable. Not like her. The green water spreads into your horses and down to your chilly bottom. Your dress of sap has never suited you. Nor does the red pen, although I find it hard to stop using to draw breasts and male genitals and bugs. Do you still fancy getting your factory walls painted? Really? Who will teach you to love unconditionally if not me? (Louise)

The Quiet

Elsie still sleeps with monsters in her bed because the beak turns her into herself.

I'm revising the Circus Pig to include a raving girl who rushes through the streets during the soon-to-be-fallen nights proclaiming an end to architecture.

I delete the incriminating parts where I plan to kill Elsie's new boyfriend, the one who dressed in my uncle's green suit.

Elderly gentlemen should not wear such white clothes in the dirt. Old gentlemen should cover their ears when the pigs trample them. Older gentlemen should wear red in the dirt. Not green. Green is the color dedicated to all dead sows.

Your face is so distorted in the silver spoon's reflection I want your mouth to be mine, your tears to be mine.

The burial place of all unwritten novels has been lost.

Elsie has turned into a pack of dogs.

Everyone loses when the factory burns down and we are no longer able to imagine the underworld.

Prayer from an occupation: This is my body. Drive the pigeons out. Abandon my stalking horse to the wilderness. Stitch by stitch.

I've been counting the bullet holes in my infamous brother to figure out how long I have to wait before I can return to the elementary school from which I still steal my language. It's still crowded. Everything is yellow and radiant.

Our tainted peepholes.

Add her nightmare seeds to the dough you knead.

The place where your grief unfolds is the place you can also call home.

Send in the political fortune seekers.

Send in the armed idealists and freed slaves.
Their time is coming now, inside my shell.
Their time shall be a cockfight.

Solemn Speech

You're not a rider, Elsie, you're a spider.

It doesn't matter what clothes you wear, what counts is how you catch the pests; at least that's what the scientist says into his microphone. Applause. When will it end? Why do my students wear such shabby clothes? Applause. I'm catching figurative rats here! Applause. I love the dimples just above your hip bone. Applause.

Can I kiss your skin folds?

Applause.

Elise, why don't you answer? Applause. Have they filled your mouth with nightmare seeds? Applause. Have they poured icing over your body? Elsie?

Note to self: This exercise is intended for humans only.

How did you slip out of your little bikini in the salt water while the German tourists lazed on the beach and my scalp burned. Oink.

It is so bright in the burial ground. I have painted my Egyptian dog the color of burned-out Chevrolets in an attempt to teach it about devotion. I'll feed it pork and let it sniff under your torn prom dress so that it can track you down in the woods later. I expose it to pork. I force you to breathe into its face. The problem is that it is too hot underground. The dog drools. I escape out onto dirt roads and minimalist color fields. Now we reach the stadium full of white people singing songs of sadness as if they were ready to join any army or crusade. Maybe they'll take care of my dog. They will not need subtitles.

You've stolen everything dark from my road movie, Shirley, and turned it into a corset. You have taken a man you despise and turned him into a cage. I know what kind of animals you want to keep. Who is the man there? How many nights does he have left? What kind of fate has Louise predicted for him? Does she sew the bodies together? Is that man you, Johannes? Is she going to turn us into cut-out burqas with swollen nipples? Is she going to melt us down and mold us into a twisted phallus? Is she going to claim that she accidentally lost us in hell and that there was no danger at all, that it was just a nice little excursion? Is she going to cast our umbilical cords in chrome? Should she reflect herself in them? Should she stuff a face with batting and claim it represents us? Is she going to bust her spider on us? What does she have in store for us? Is Shirley our salvation?

The balloon with the black sun lands on my chest. The Junk poet burns the balloon with his lighter and the splinter from the black sun penetrates my heart. Applause. Curtain.

AFTER THE PERFORATION, MORE PERFORATION

There inside. It's not broken enough. Where. Inside. That's why we continued to fuck. That was the only reason to keep fucking. That's the only reason to fuck. Because we weren't broken enough yet. We staged the brilliant cuckoo with our hands tied above our heads. We staged the angry cuckoo pressed against the wall. Twit-twit-twit jug-jug-jug. We staged the crushed cuckoo against the window. We staged the leaking cuckoo. We staged the cute cuckoo. We wanted to throw the gates wide open for the cuckoo but now the cuckoo is pecking at our skin. It wants to come back.

Applause.

Shirley. It was Shirley who called. The desert king immediately went off on his moped to pick her up. She thought he was a Danish storyteller, but it wasn't him, it was a fairytale Scheherazade from *One Thousand and One Nights* who adores Mayakovsky and fat girls. He pronounces all his poems out loud, with a red hole for a mouth.

Shirley is not very fat so she needs to hurry and put on some weight now. She acquaints herself with plastic toys and cat pee and just yearns for her lover every other day.

One day Shirley goes to visit the imprisoned lover. She smuggles some junk in her pussy. They fuck "unsupervised" on a bunk bed. It isn't very sexy. She thinks she probably doesn't love him anymore. The guard grins as he holds the door open for her, probably thinking he will watch their dry intercourse through his peephole. She hurries back to the sandbox. She learns to love the Junk Poet too in her own strange little way, and he loves her too, in his own little way, even though she was never very fat.

And the dead continue to flow out of her cunt and die like spilled stinking junk, landing, in this timeless space, on the sticky surface of the factory floor. And the sand in the sandbox is so cold. It continues to be so cold. That's where her grave was, right from the start. It was always there.

Elsie looks fatally otherworldly in the blue glow. Elsie is slowly on her way to her own demise. Elsie uses the shards from the broken window. Shirley has to play Elsie doing a Louise. She has to do it to honor all the dead lovers. They deserve an otherworldly girlfriend in blue light. They deserve a woman who portrays a broken mother. They deserve a woman who can't stop doing drugs, but strangely manages to stay alive. She is a blue glow inhaler. She continues to live. She spreads her legs on the factory floor and gives birth to death. Also it is a cliché to reproduce on the factory floor that has already smelled everything.

SHIRLEY IS THE ANSWER TO ALL CORRUPT POEMS

Shirley was born in Santa Monica, California in 1928. Shirley died in 2014 in Woodside, California. During the 1930s, she was one of the biggest stars in film. It is likely that her films saved several movie studios from bankruptcy. Will you save us from the sorrow that Louise forces upon us, Shirley? Can you play little girl for us? Shirley, in all the title tracks of your films you are referred to as little. Shirley, have you always been a little girl? Shirley, are you still a little girl? Shirley, we want to see your curls dance on your head like a shiny halo. Sorrow is an insect that gnaws at the heart. We can't live without this nagging. I see clearly when I am drawn down into the green lake of melancholy. Let me remain on the bottom of this green lake.

At first, your daughter seems unbreakable. Still, she breaks down. I read in a book where someone's face is described as broken, worn away. To have one's face described in that way must be the greatest of insults, no not insult, rather tyrannical ruthlessness, to have someone's rude dominion hurled at one's (broken) face like that.

Every day I try to put make-up over the face I wear, which in the book is described as broken, worn away. For a very long time I was taken to be much younger than I was. It was because my face still belonged to a child, even when I was on heroin my face belonged to a child. It is the longing for the first wafer and all those who have died and continue to die that has turned my face into something broken, worn away.

My freckles have turned into bullet spots. My colander is dirty. I'm going to do Shirley's make-up. I'll do the Shirley if you promise not to laugh. Excuse me, I'm just going to go make up the longing on my face, excuse me, I'm just going to go make up the mental obsession off my face, excuse me. You should do that too, Johannes. Get your daughter's makeup off your face. Just stare into your own face when the reflection is polished and your face is bare. Lock yourself in the bathroom. Stay there.

Give me stranglers and ex-girlfriends

Give me intruders and explicit narratives

Give me broken chamber music

Give me the kind of romance that takes place in a pawn shop

Give me my stalkers and those who always forgive

Give me breeders

Give me a mountain blaster

Give me the infected song we sang

Give me the world without horses we always sing about

Give me the bleeding woman who barks

Give me burning pictures that should have been buried

Give me the spiders of the mother tongue

Give me father's mouth

Give me humps

THE ISLAND OF DEATH

My daughter keeps her eyes closed
as I pick the chips out of her rocking horse.

She belongs to Louise now.

All I own is revenge.

Johannes, I didn't believe you when you said that the desert landscape was part of her body, a dangerous and maybe even scandalous part of her body, that secret area of the body could lead you back the paranoia or the opera. Right Johannes? Where are you? In the paranoia or at the opera? In the front row? It was you who wrote that since the beginning of time, daughters have wanted to cut their father's throat. Have you looked at yourself long enough in the mirror, Johannes? You already belong to my dominion, no words are needed to be spoken aloud.

You are sneaky and quick at night as LA glows with light as it burns to the ground. You need this charade lit by flashlights. You need boots to march in. You need a new bruise for your thigh. Do you want to taste the needle? If I give you my first wafer, it will be your last. Shirley's curls are a halo. Her non-alcoholic drink contains two parts gasoline. Shirley says: You need me and my tainted expression if you're ever going to leave this quarantine. The text is a crypt for the past and the future. The text is a grave. The text is a prediction. Greetings Kassandra! When can we go home, Kassandra?

Louise, the factory
The Louise Factory

Louise has decorated the factory walls with headlines from evening papers, clippings from gossip magazines, reproductions from art books. The floor is covered in garbage. Beneath the inept machines: half-eaten freezer meals, candy wrappers, beer cans, plastic cutlery, doll eyes, thumbtacks, wafers, spider legs, interrupted sunbeams, strained mud from the green bottom of the green lake. It's the 32nd night. Eight left to go.

Shirley hasn't cleaned. Shirley is stuck in the scrub. Louise has nailed a thousand and one nights to her walls. In particular, on the door to Shirley's scrub. Louise has divided our nights into forty sections. That's how long it takes for us to turn into expired spray. If the spray doesn't swallow us. Forty nights is the time required to determine whether we have been affected by the disease.

We still don't know the name of the disease. We think the disease has the same name as the drink named after Shirley. We have cherry pits in our mouths, the flesh is gnawed away with the help of our charred canines. Soon we will be grilled like wounded pigs.

You imagine that the disease is me because I am foreign, because I am a mother and therefore symbolizes birth and death. But I am not the disease. You are the disease. The only thing that is foreign here is you, in front of yourselves. You imagine that I store your dead memories. You imagine that Shirley is free of similes, that she is the swarm, the makeup that accentuates your broken face. Are you so afraid of getting stuck in the fortieth night? You have opened the door to the allegory. But the door to the quarantine is still kept closed. She is so grim, that woman.

Louise and her theatre. Louise and her factory floor. Louise and the walls. Louise and her speech. She calls it "hide and seek". She plays my husband. She plays your wife. She plays your dead daughter. She plays my dead lover. She plays my miscarriage. She plays dead. Never mind her, bitch, we're moving on. Don't worry about her, Johannes. She talks so much shit. Do not be sad. Your daughter has drops of sweat tattooed on her inner thigh. She calls the tattoo "my little squeaking birds". At the beginning of the poem, you gave me a tattoo of a female spider on my thigh. It's gone now.

I call this part of the poem "The Swimming Pool", even though I don't have chlorine in my eyes yet, even though it is actually called "The Island of Death".

From the hallway, we can hear Shirley (it was she who tricked us into the swarm, it was she who diverted one poem from another, it was she who washed the girls in gasoline and put chlorine in our eyes) whisper: I picked up the horse skeletons from a beach. I never removed the rabies virus from your eyes. Don't mind my neck. I have already sold it to the highest bidder, a WW2 necklace maker. The film crew suffers from a skin disease. I've known that all along. It's almost dawn. There is the hastily covered-up doorway. Every word fits on the wall. I'm still stuck in the hallway. We are alone in the guest room. I hope you brought our props with you. Your faces are still broken. Sara, you will turn into a spoon woman and Johannes, you will own all eight severed spider legs. It is too dangerous for us to leave. That's the only thing Louise has tried to say this whole time. That leaving is a dangerous mission. It's more dangerous out there than in here.

"Island of Death" after Arnold Böcklin's painting.

Who is dressed in white and who is dressed in black? Who sits down and who stands up? Who shits openly in nature?

The synthetic woman has always had her origin on the "Island of Death." Behind the walls hide the red fields. It is from this place that all literature unfolds.

Here's the swarm.

Six more nights.

The next part of the poem is called "Rise". It's because I love the song "Rise." "Rise" contains encrypted text, dirty highways, wide open windows, chilled skin, cigarette smoke. It's about a girl who thinks she's a mass murderer and a boy who belongs to the lost. Let's see if they can survive out there. Let's kiss each other with open mouths. Let's see if the boy can keep the girl safe. The boy breaks the bike locks with a circular saw he stole from Biltema. The chips flash in the girl's apartment. The boy and the girl sell their stolen bikes for SEK 350 each. If they sell three pieces per day, they stay above the surface. It's even enough for a chocolate cake with coconut flavor and clean panties at Lindex sale.

Let's see who can breathe through the plastic. The plastic mask has tears instead of eyes and no mouth. It looks like our salvation. Let's see if it is. Let's see what kind of house they built using this deck. Let's see nothing. No, don't show me. I'm afraid of houses. But the islands have never scared me.

REVENGE

The boy dies. The girl devotes herself to longing for him. He crawls around down on the deep green bottom of the lake. Watch how her longing overtakes her whole life, how it transforms her into a monotonous fantasy, how it crowds out everything else. Days added to nights and nights added to days, weeks added to years. It's not forty nights, it's almost forty years. She clings to the flow that was once injected into her blood, the pale yellow flowing into her like a line of girls. Watch them dance arm-in-arm into her body! And how they can't find their way out. They are stuck in a longing, a monotonous fantasy, an obsession, a disease. Is it a curse? Is it also the curse of writing? To continue fattening the thoughts, the streams of honey, time and time again compulsively imagining the sweetness and the clear, bright yellow flow in the veins? In the middle of the day, the girl clings to the memory of the perfect, flawless state, which is completely absolute in her own formless body.

Is that Shirley's green body? Who buried it? Who digs it up again?

WE'LL CARVE YOU LIKE YOU'RE ON FIRE

I want my own banged-up place in the sun, but my eyes feel too feathery and the empty phrases I arrive through are always too raw. I want my own underage girls in piles of shoveled sand. I want to be the mistress of the ritual re-creation of my own lost body parts. The girls fall off their bikes. Because their longing is too strong. They're riding their bikes. They yearn. They fall. They long for sun. They yearn for an existence encompassed by sun, to be in the middle of it, but still not. A sunlike existence, but without the light of the sun. Their bikes were stolen. I sold them to them for twice the price. I lived on it for over two days.

It is whispered: in every fury there is a seed of absolute silence. And she, the girl with whom the poem has suddenly become so preoccupied, has found her seed, her murdered gold. She intends to cling to it, protect it, preserve it until her need for protection turns into nervous illness. She's never going to let go of it. This stillness. This bath. Her seed. Her holy seed. Her nightmare seed.

My film crew still thinks this poem is about makeup and a heart that doesn't beat. The girls fell from their bikes and instantly begin to freeze on the Central Station's concrete floor. Someone gives them a blanket. As we discuss my slurred coronations of underworld figures, it's important to pay attention to wasps and needles. It's important to understand girls, their cold bodies.

No I don't know if the green helps, no I don't know if the decorations of the underworld could constitute our salvation, no I don't know if the makeup we throw over the dead makes any difference. It's probably all in vain. Anything you write in the real world only ends up imprisoning you. Your revival stories are sacred nightmare seeds. Nibble them up for me. Three more nights.

THE REVENGE OF
THE DESERT KING

[The leaden figures are huddled along the foundation of the house, what are they actually trying to imitate? They have never been very good actors. Their expressions are tone-deaf, emotionless. Our box is full of mud and still over-flowing with plastic toys. The Junk Poet has got a new hat. He got it from a woman who was chubbier than Shirley. It's nice. Shirley has dyed her hair red. Maybe they've got bedsores from their desert trek, but they haven't yet lifted their clothes to check. The makeup has long since washed off their faces. The eyes are lakes and their mouths are secret springs.]

SHIRLEY: If I didn't have such perfect nails, would you still be singing with me?

THE JUNK POET: I don't sing.

SHIRLEY: Would you use a hammer?

THE JUNK POET: Stop naming your weapons. Your boyfriend sawed off my finger with a circular saw. He thought I was attracted to you. It's absurd. He thinks I should leave you alone. I told him you can do exactly what you want.

SHIRLEY: He's inside.

THE JUNK POET: Then he is the one who uses the hammer.

SHIRLEY: And I was left alone. I'm always left alone. I'm tired. I don't want to sit in your sandbox anymore. I'm so lonely. God, I'm so lonely.

THE JUNNK POET: So leave.

SHIRLEY: Don't you love me anymore?

THE JUNK POET: Love has nothing to do with this.

SHIRLEY: But I'm all you have, right now, in this moment.

THE JUNK POET: Is that what you think? Someone else will come along soon enough. In my sandbox, the visits never end. The visitors are my livelihood. You too are a visitor.

SHIRLEY: Will the fortieth night end on a note?

THE JUNK POET: I am not Jesus wandering through the desert. No devil tempts me. I'm already a wreck. You know that I have poems in my head, that my mouth is the only tool I use to spread my poems.

SHIRLEY: Your body is fabulous. I can't bear to listen to it anymore.

THE JUNK POET: It was not I who decided that the probationary period should be forty nights. It was God.

SHIRLEY: What country are you *from*?

THE JUNK POET: I swallowed a grain of sand and the sandbox became my home. It will continue to rain because that's what God and his horses have decided.

SHIRLEY: I don't want to listen to your universe anymore.

THE JUNK POET: Then leave. The cats are screaming. The disposable cutlery is all I need.

SHIRLEY: Stop! You are sent by God to take care of me. That is your purpose in the world. My boyfriend sawed off your finger because of me and now we are forever linked. The horse skeleton has been vandalized. The basement is obscene. The police heard that I spent hours interrogating cockroaches about God. I found out about gravity by fucking an ophthalmologist in Borlänge. The symbolism is redundant. Your words are a jacket full of swans. They burst out.

THE JUNK POET: But leave then, just leave. I have no use for you anymore. Never had any use for you. You became a poem, and nothing more. You're too skinny for me. I can't suck any words out of your pitiful tits. I never planned for you to be part of the forty days. God can chop off all my ten fingers and all ten toes and it still won't have anything to do with you, even if it's your boyfriend doing the actual mutilation. God did not promise to give you to me as a gift. I have to get ready. Leave.

SHIRLEY: What are we getting ready for?

THE JUNK POET: Leave, just leave.

SHIRLEY: You and my boyfriend knew each other long before I came into the picture. I'm just a pawn in your game. What did you even need me for?

THE JUNK POET: Don't raise yourself to the skies now. Don't exaggerate so much you soil yourself.

[The rain stops falling and the clouds crack apart from the new radiant light and the new beginning is unexpectedly here: this is our tremendously moment of clarity, the height of melancholy, the first day that preceded the last night, the new world of the radiant sun. The sunrays move like lightning across the earth's crust, cleaving it in two in a single brilliant moment. The sun shines, and destroys, and it touches everything, it destroys everything, just everything, from horizon to horizon.

It touches Johannes and Shirley and Louise and Elsie and Calypso and Sara and Great Uncle and Kassandra and all the dead it feigns the shadows of the green mothers and at the same moment, it becomes nourishment for everyone involved.]

POSTCARDS

Dear Johannes,

The island of death is still populated by women in tunics. We collect the parts of death's wreckage as they wash up on the beach. The skeleton of a whale becomes our talisman. The new sun burns our skulls to ashes. We are supported by the mother tongue. We dress up in skirts. It's possible to describe us as fake, but that still doesn't bother us.

Dear Johannes,

I whispered into the shell and came into existence. Then I played with my fragile marbles. I moved them in a row on top of each other so that they finally formed a string of pearls around me in the quicksand of the artificial island. When I removed the marbles, one by one, they left small depressions in the sand. The circular shape of nothingness. In every little depression, my little self screamed. When I was removed from the island, I left one last depression: the shape of my body. I've screamed goodbye to that beautiful, bone-white beach. Who will welcome me into the city?

Dear Sara,

I am covered in snow.
I am covered in snow.
and it's laying its eggs
in the most embarrassing
parts of my body.

Dear Johannes,

Everything turned into someone else's leftovers. The chest is heavy and full of sand. Everything is wrapped in the blanket of sticky cobwebs. Nothing gets out.

Dear Sara,
Popped some sleeping pills
and crawled back
into bed with Cassandra.

Dear Johannes,
You don't want to die in a city where you can't even live, wrote the German poet who himself was run over by a car. I could die in this town, but only if a big truck plowed over me. My shoulders would buckle and my ribcage would break.

Dear Sara,
Sometimes I think I was a truck in my past life.
Sometimes I think I was German.

Dear Johannes,
All this stillness inside me, it's killing me. All this eternity inside me, it kills me. There is no time left to wait.

Dear Sara,
The snow is in my hair.
My hands are crossed across my chest
and my body is being used by something that is not me.

Dear Johannes,
Today I saw a truck parked on the country road next to a field full of dried leftover barley. If I would have looked into the backseat, I might have thought the truck belonged to a lover because of the broken glass, or a barber because of the scissors, or a fool because of the torn letters, or a child because the guns weren't loaded yet. Sometimes I think I'm a truck that crushed a chest. Sometimes I think I am the chest.

Dear Sara,

An archaic child sleeps inside me. I am the guard on the beach who saves the other children. Your truck keeps on driving off the bridges. The animals inside the truck keep drowning.

Dear Johannes,

My truck is stuck at the muddy bottom of the lake and nobody owns a submarine that goes this far beneath the skin.

Dear Sara,

I am the scalding hot water in your dirty bathtub. I am impossible time. I am a luminescent shard of the moon lost from time. Now you are walled in the city. The cement mixer is the world inside me. All journeys go backwards from now on.

Dear Johannes,

It was Shirley who wrote this poem on the walls:
You were a human before devastation turned you into a human.

Dear Sara,

You're a real joker in a town full of people who hurt me when they try to smile. I've noticed how you mimic my days by standing still. I have seen you imitate my ways by beating in the wind. I hear you imitating my daughter as I try in vain to fall asleep.

Dear Johannes,

The only thing left is to live with your kidnapped and made-up soul. Your hunt leads you down.

Dear Mom,
I thought I was in love, but then I found out
that it was bipolar disorder.
Don't ask me how it feels. Put the cigarette out
on my thigh.

Dear Dad,
I feel good.

Dear Lovely Sunday Ignition,
I will always remember your porn and your cold coffee.
I will always remember your floor and your chest.

Dear Calypso,
Don't wait for us.

THE LAST INSTRUMENT

The speed of the horses. The steel of cars. The black of lightning. The glass of hands. The steam of skin. Scars of lips. The dance of morning dew. Night of teeth. Road of sand. The path of rawness. Wheel of stars. The breakdown of the skin. The kiss of the stars. The tyrant of the blue breast. The courage of the screws. The small space between huge and big. The small distance between here and there. The naked snare grows out of the clothes. Dance of powdery mildew. That's the only way you learn how to play the instrument you wear around your neck. Spring is almost over. The apple blossoms are poisonous. Great Uncle is a science fiction novel. Louise is your fantasy of the Eternal Mothers. The daughters are the holes in the underworld. Spasms of powdery mildew. The darkness of the sun. Cobweb epilepsy. The translation of death. Shirley's wig. The paradise of silver spoons. Dig us a hole.

THE FINAL NIGHT

On the final day, it is the shadows that shine the brightest, it is the shadows that generate the necessary heat. The shadows still offer hiding places, the shadows create a haven for artificial light, the yellowish shimmer, the sickly shimmer, the very quiet and murky light, the kind of light that turns bruises and puncture wounds into warm flowers. The red flowers spread across the factory floor, the blood poems congeal and Shirley has escaped, she is not going to mop up Louise's factory floor anymore.

There she is, Louise. I am a labyrinthine garden of wives and dead daughters, she says. King Bloom. The quarantine is the sixth and as yet unknown version of Arnold Böcklin's "Island of Death". It was dug up from a factory floor. It is a vehicle of the night. The window is blank, the sky mottled, and the trees look very thin. Since you are a landscape painter, you are also a kleptomaniac. On the island, everything I say sounds ekphrastic. I do my best imitation of an echo in this wheelbarrow: I chew dried meat. I try to understand why the birth records are so incompletely filled out.

Eurydice's father ate salt. The lullaby Louise sings to the spiders has been deleted. *Imse vimse spider* goes the song. What surprise is waiting for us now? Outside: a garden with birds (sparrows). I can't find a single feather here. My torso is cleansed. Everywhere there's snow.

Please, Melee, just because you're my sister doesn't mean I won't be shaking like a burning tree during the next children's crusade. Please, jackal-hearted masses, erect a statue to commemorate the red hands of thieves who taught me all I know about tenderness. Please, hypothermia, whose mirror are we stepping into now?

In the shadow, servants offer golden orange drinks. No more wars. Just this. Yellow soldier girls in mortal combat, prisoners of war with their mouths sewn shut, your own witch trial, the little prostitutes, ventriloquists and nodding dolls, whispers in your veins, deformed soot skulls, this obliteration of yourself. I have touched something inside you and you were swept away. You let me touch you. We are inextricably bound to each other now. Says Louise.

The taxidermist has become a representative of all that is lovable about language breaks. Customization has turned into a supermarket feeder. Right away: My joy! The Kleptomaniac's Melody. The pumpkin lantern is used to shoot deer in the forest. Dry leaves crackle underfoot. I have to make it to the end of the week, before the turns are taken out in the display cabinet, before the herd is released. Apart from my museum, I know nothing about underwear or wild escape. I can't live in here unless I can tame the pale stain on my window.

Johannes, do the Louise for me.

You must know – you who deal with fairy tales, myths and monsters, you who stick faces on the walls – that the violence in fiction never exceeds the violence in reality? And that's why you might as well bury yourself in exaggerations. You know they are as real as the real violence and that paradise is where you get killed. It's where the spear is thrown and the heart is stabbed.

But don't look so damn surprised!

(This story lives on its own hyperbole.)

Let's burn down the factory. Before Louise comes and showers us with
red flowers.

I probably know what Louise does. Yes. This is Louise's truth: she wants you to fall in love with her. Since you have no memory, you are an empty vessel for her to fill. Because your self-produced chemical body fills you with terror. She knows you are in dire need of a skilled chemist. She knows that you read your own lack and your own need into everything irrational and twisted, she says, that everything turns into the search for the manual that can make you understand your own flawed body, that your whole life has consisted of that the search, that you read signs everywhere to check and read your own chemical imbalance, the disease that makes you a mutilated idiot. She knows about all that. That's why she's here now. This is Louise's collection, her prison of bluebells.

Have you shaved your head enough?

Junk Song

Everything grunts joink joink
track the turkey
follow the last cold powder
from the mind's cold
war with the cold body
puke out the thigh bone
the senses are wrecked
by a war inside the inner
ear island
death's island has exploded
from a nymph bomb
wrecks strewn on the beach
on my inner thigh
there are worms
on my inner turkey thighs
joink joink chew up
the bombazine

The shimmering oasis is extremely toxic with its ancient water. The evaporation over thousands of years has made the water extremely salty. Do you see the swarm? Shirley's painted face? All these flies circling above the poisoned pool. And there! The swallows! They make it, almost always they make it, because they manage to get the liquid they need from the bodies of the flies. Thanks to the flies, they survive.

Some of the flies suffer from heat stroke, falling mutely to the ground. Do you hear? Listen carefully. When it gets too hot, the sand moans, the friction between the grains of sand makes the whole landscape sound and move.

The singing dunes of the desert.

It hasn't always looked so pitiful. There are remnants of the landscape before the world turned into this miserable sand: segments of the world's largest lake, ruins of human civilization, patches of green grass, limestone formations, not-yet-dried tears. Dung beetles scurry around your dehydrated body. Look over there! Little silver ants scurry in the scorching, look! That one grabs a fainted fly, watch how it purposefully disassembles its insect parts to bring the whole body with it.

I don't remember where I'm from myself but I know she's from an island pronounced Oh-Yeah-Yeah. I know that there was once a light, but that everything is reduced to bubblegum suns. I know that most things fall apart as soon as they are examined under a magnifying glass. My own broken face deceives myself into thinking it practices ignorance. Tell me, what else is it going to do?

That is her face which is my face, burnt to pieces, tanned by the scorching sun, waxy, like dried mud, only this dry skin of hers most like a death mask. A death mask that is a decoction of her once living face. It is no longer the memory of her beloved that drives her forward. It is the death mask that drives her forward, that petrified face that still wanders around in its own desert on *The Island of Death*.

The wall cools my ear. The train thumps close. It takes me to the horizon. A monastery claimed in the news press that they had part of Jesus' foreskin. This poem claims to be the final version of *The Island of Death*.

Are you the bomb

No I am the island

POSTCARDS

johannes

a new quarantine will take my place is your debut book from 2007 and is the basic construction for our many mouths in this work

johannes

mother tongue, the mouths

johannes

the text speaks our common mother tongue. a mother is green in the poem. she is locked in quarantine. the text babbles the mother tongue while echoing the mother tongue in exile. the native language is here and the native language is there and the text babbles foreign phrases. from the beginning we misunderstood each other. our vain attempts to make sounds intelligible. our quarantine speaks many tongues. perhaps most of all the tongues speak the language of sorrow, the language of love, the language of beasts, the language of confusion. the language of obsession, the language of the incomprehensible. a crow for you. the night mouths. don't try to understand me. aim the blowtorch at your-self instead. we meet in our simple attempts to light up the mouth of darkness

johannes

did the green mother in the poem start speaking with her night mouth when we imprisoned her in the quarantine cave or did she speak like that from the beginning?

johannes

there is something chewed-up and worn-out about *a new quarantine*
and that is what whispers and invites and shouts to me that I too am
part of the chewed-up and worn-out inside the quarantine

blame yourself johannes

you were the one who started this

johannes

we have about forty days to finish this

johannes

while I was writing I often thought of Arachne even though she wasn't
there when you wrote *a new quarantine* but the news about her reached
me while I was here, writing inside your infection barrier, I stayed inside
quarantine and continued to write about your dead daughter. at the
same time: the news of the ex-lover's death reached me. now they have
been entwined.

johannes

it is always the jailer of words who is the real prisoner

johannes

is literature a valve through which reality breathes

or

is it the other way around?

johannes

Arachne is present in words such as death, infant, spider's leg, web, web

my lover is present in words like death, spoon, poison, murder

remove exactly what you want though

i'm going to count every word you remove

and collect them

in another book

johannes

our dead worlds and living dungeons (mythologies and realities) have
become a blanket woven of spider thread and now we sweep it over
quarantine

quarantine's funeral

johannes

maybe Arachne and the dead lover don't belong together

but in quarantine they are forced to share the same room

I have written everything in your quarantine

I made everything mine

also the ongoing reality that is constantly plowing over bones

I made it mine

johannes

literature does not sit and wait for permission

johannes

you were the one who created the quarantine. it was you who created a book out of the already poisoned

johannes

you emigrated to the united states when you were in the borderland between adolescence and childhood. you were thirteen the year was 1986. I was five years old then and could neither read nor write so therefore I have no diary entries from that year.

a new quarantine was published on december 1, 2007 and from december 1, 2007 I have a diary entry and it reads: "why does my vocabulary feel so poor? why don't I write about the gang rape in the basement? about chihuahua who lost its breath? why don't I write about the new? I just lie in bed next to my husband. well into the morning in a darkened room."

industrious braids, rectal wire root, rascal young

johannes

what did you write in your diary in 1986?

johannes placing a spider trapped in the quarantine was a prerequisite. the spider is our script's terminator.

johannes I translate your quarantine in google translate

I run every word combination you wrote in a new quarantine through a mechanical filter that may or may not have a digital long-term memory. johannes a new quarantine will take my place is fed through the text machine google translate which is based on probabilities and in this way the end product becomes, maybe or maybe not, a paradox. google translate makes its own choices and controls my translation and from the syntactic error I continue working with your quarantine.

johannes

google translate will take your place

johannes

translation means defilement and it is quite so beautiful

johannes

our leaking long-term memory

johannes

translation is always naive and intimate and selfish and must always mean more to the translator than to the translated

johannes

the first time we met was *ett lysande namn,* the online magazine. the year was 2010. your poem was called *the quarantine unit* and I made an automania of the quarantine unit. viktor johansson was the one who opened our separate mouths. we are back at square zero. quarantine is the ground zero of our common writing. the aggregate is our method

johannes

this postcard is not an apology

at that time I was always very brief in my emails because I was doing drugs and stuck in my own quarantine and didn't want my failed reasoning to be visible to you

I repeat

this postcard is not an apology

johannes

you never made a point of my terse emails or no emails at all you always replied just as tersely you never demanded a word from my brain (intellect) only from my heart (literature)

I am grateful for that

it is only in this way that the crow's song continues

johannes

this is perhaps the first time we correspond

johannes

this is not correspondence these are postcards sent to myself where i call myself johannes

johannes

i'm not waiting for you to throw out the thread, our work has already woven its threads, the blanket has already been spread over cellular tissue and death, the work goes on regardless

johannes

so many ghostly voices rattling. so many mouths buried in the earth. I take the spoon and dig. yes we use the spoons from the postcards. don't let anyone see your real face when you remove the spoon from your face. when you remove the spoon from your face let them see the face that has already received a thousand mouths

johannes

what part of the spoon do you use when you dig?

convex or concave. reduced or enlarged. always distorted? when the words are mirrored on both sides of the spoon

johannes
digging in the earth with a spoon is also a work of translation. how many votes do we manage to unearth? the earth is full of contaminated seeds. we pick them out with our new beaks. what is written in the sand?

nightmare seeds

johannes

with a spoon / he dug out the crocodiles' eyes / and slapped the monkeys behind. / with a spoon.

federico garcía lorca

johannes
a new quarantine will take your place

johannes

I write a postcard that is the back text of the quarantine. I will send it
another day.

johannes

the mouth has a sore

all mouths have sores

not just the night mouth

even though it's the night mouth that babbles and babbles and

despite the green lady standing there

still standing

where

and curtsies and say that now it is ours

johannes

today I didn't want to write a postcard

Dear Sara Tuss,

I'm finally finishing our book. It's making me sick. I might have caught something from my children, but I think it's our book that's making me sick. It took us years to write, and it's taking me years to edit down to one book. I can't do it. There are too many stories, too many games, too many characters. I'm like one of those drug-addled boomer directors who loose track of the budget and keep filming. I don't have a budget but I keep filming. Even though all the actors have left the forest, I'm still filming. Not selfies but otheries, as you demanded from me when we first met in this underworld we called The Quarantine.

We joined together a quarantine, an old underground world I created twenty years ago. And there we lost our voices. We played dress-up. We disguised ourselves and through our disguises we created a new book, which I am now finishing while sick in bed.

In the quarantine, we abandoned the traditional roles of translator and author, we abandoned the conventional model of original and translation. Our voices didn't blend but they became brackish.

Traditions exist for a reason. Without it the book grew and grew until we no longer knew where it began and ended, no longer could tell where Sara Tuss began and Shirley ended, no longer could tell if Johannes was in the quarantine or if he'd been replaced by a junkie poet, an angel, a dizzy child. Translation has to be watched or it will ruin the quarantine. Texts will leak, become uncontainable.

Well, Sara Tuss, I want to write this to you to tell you I've finished our game of Anti-death, I've put a stop to the filming. Now I'm barricading the doors to the quarantine. It will take our place.

Love,
Johannes

Thanks to Mike Corrao for wrestling this thing into book form. Thanks Joyelle McSweeney and James Pate for help editing it. Thanks to Seedlings. Thanks to Mo(o)on Books (editors Noah Ross and 최 Lindsay) or publishing an excerpt as a chapbook, and Berkeley Poetry Review/Ordkonst (editors 최 Lindsay and Erik Isberg) and Seedling (editor Jerrold Shiroma) for publishing excerpts in issues of their journals. Thanks to Mark Tursi and Richard Greeenfield who published the first version of the book with Apostrophe Books back in 2007 and thanks to John Trefry for publishing the new version.

Johannes Göransson is the author of nine previous books of poetry and criticism, including *Poetry Against All, Summer* and *Transgressive Circulation: Essays on Translation*, and has translated numerous poets, including Aase Berg, Ann Jäderlund, Eva Kristina Olsson, Helena Boberg and Kim Yideum. His poems, translations and critical writings have appeared in a wide array of journals in the US and broad, including *Fence, Poetry Magazine, Lana Turner,* and *Spoon River Review.* He is a professor at the University of Notre Dame and the publisher of Action Books.

Sara Tuss Efrik (b. 1981) is a writer and performance artist from Sweden. She has an MFA in theater from the Theater Academy in Malmö and has studied at The Nordic Writing School at Biskops-Arnö. Her 2012 debut novel was *Mumieland.* Her performance piece *Mother Dog* was recently staged at the Gothenburg City Theater. In the US, she has published two chapbooks: *Automanias: Selected Poems* (Goodmorning Menagerie, 2016)—winner of the 2015 Goodmorning Menagerie Chapbook-in-Translation contest—and *The Night's Belly* (Toad Press, 2016), both translated by Paul Cunningham. She has also just finished her second novel, *Nobody is sick, nobody is dirty, nobody is dead.*

www.ingramcontent.com/pod-product-compliance
Lightning Source LLC
Chambersburg PA
CBHW041147300726
48978CB00017B/1410